A Candlelight Ecstasy Romance®

"DON'T GO, GRANT . . ."

His voice was hoarse. "I'll stay as long as you need me." In the next moment his lips covered hers in a hard, demanding, fiery kiss. Gone was the gentle, playful caressing as his rugged masculine desire overtook them both. His strong arms engulfed her, pulling her completely to him, molding her to his hard, virile body. His lips sent pangs of passion shooting through her limbs. The moments hung like eternity and she was lost in his arms, in his animal magnetism, in his kiss. . . .

A CANDLELIGHT ECSTASY ROMANCE ®

LEGACY
OF LOVE

Tate McKenna

A CANDLELIGHT ECSTASY ROMANCE ®

Published by
Dell Publishing Co., Inc.
1 Dag Hammarskjold Plaza
New York, New York 10017

Copyright © 1983 by Mary Tate Engels

All rights reserved. No part of this book may be
reproduced or transmitted in any form or by any
means, electronic or mechanical, including photocopying,
recording or by any information storage
and retrieval system, without the written permission
of the Publisher, except where permitted by law.

Dell ® TM 681510, Dell Publishing Co., Inc.

Candlelight Ecstasy Romance®, 1,203,540, is a registered
trademark of Dell Publishing Co., Inc., New York, New
York.

ISBN: 0-440-15096-5

Printed in the United States of America
First printing—March 1983

To Noel, Brent, & Shane, who inspire my life

To Our Readers:

We have been delighted with your enthusiastic response to Candlelight Ecstasy Romances® and we thank you for the interest you have shown in this exciting series.

In the upcoming months we will continue to present the distinctive sensuous love stories you have come to expect only from Ecstasy. We look forward to bringing you many more books from your favorite authors and also the very finest work from new authors of contemporary romantic fiction.

As always we are striving to present the unique absorbing love stories that you enjoy most—books that are more than ordinary romance.

Your suggestions and comments are always welcome. Please write to us at the address below.

Sincerely,

The Editors
Candlelight Romances
1 Dag Hammarskjold Plaza
New York, N.Y. 10017

CHAPTER ONE

"Damn! Why would Daddy do a thing like this to me?" Morgan kicked stubbornly at the sturdy Colorado-rock fireplace, as if the blow would diminish her wrath. A merrily crackling fire dispelled the early April chill, but not the frigid tension in the room.

Her oldest brother, Brett, chuckled mercilessly. "To legitimatize you, little sis. He was just old-fashioned enough to want his darling daughter to be married before she lives with a man!"

Morgan struggled to restrain the urge to slap him. In years past she wouldn't have resisted, but at twenty-five she was a child no longer. Instead she opposed him angrily. "I didn't live with— Oh, what's the use? Damn you, Brett! I'll bet you had something to do with this! As the official lawyer in the family, you helped Daddy draw up the will. It's a male chauvinistic deed! How could you do this to me? Your own sister!"

A fleeting glance of pity crossed Brett's golden eyes as he professed with candor, "Morgan, I—believe it or not—I didn't have anything to do with it. This was all Dad's crazy idea. Honest to God, it was! There was nothing I could do about it. He was adamant. Why would I—"

Her tawny brown eyes spit fire at him as she interrupted. "I don't believe you! You just want to get all the family's property in the hands of the men! You and Adam!"

He threw his hands in exasperation. "Morgan, be sensible. I have all the property I can possibly say grace over. And I of all

11

people wouldn't force anyone into marriage. God knows, I wouldn't do that. I don't care what you do—or who you do it with!"

"There you go again!" Morgan insisted.

"Look, honey. How do you think it looked to Dad when you traveled all over Europe with a mixed group of men and women? He knew what you were up to! He was no fool, just old-fashioned."

"But we were just friends. We didn't—"

"And then you went to Greece alone with André? Come on, Morgana dear. Be reasonable. How much innocence did you expect Dad to swallow?"

"But why did he want to make it a part of his will? What does having a husband have to do with keeping that stupid, run-down ranch property?" It was beyond her understanding.

"Because he felt that it would take a man to make a go of any ranch." Why did Brett sound like her father when he said that?

"Well, I'll show you . . . all of you! I'll make it work, by myself!" Morgan folded her arms defiantly, hugging her chilled body in the process. She wore a creamy turtleneck sweater that clung to the swell of her breasts and tucked into the trim waist of her tan tweed skirt. The deep brown velveteen blazer matched the sable of her exquisite eyes and contrasted sharply with her golden crown. The long, silky-blond tresses were tucked into a noble chignon, befitting the austerity of the day. There was an air of richness—of class—in her attire, but actually Morgan couldn't wait to get back into casual clothes and let her hair down.

"You'll make it work?" Brett's laugh was a sneer. "What do you know about ranching? You grew up in Denver's suburbs. The only ranch you know about is a dude ranch!"

A determined expression spread across Morgan's face, lighting her spicy brown eyes and radiating her creamy complexion. "Then that's what I'll do with it. I'll turn it into a dude ranch! And I'll make it profitable. Then what'll you do about it, Mr. Bigshot Lawyer? Do you think that'll settle the will . . . or will you devise another way to get that property for yourself?"

Brett glared at her with a satisfied smirk. "Don't forget about the stipulation to be married within a year."

12

"Well, at least I have twelve months to accomplish that! I'll worry about it later."

"Worry about what later?" Adam, the third Cassity sibling, entered the room. Sensing the friction, he didn't wait for an answer. "What's going on between you two?"

"Little sis is upset over Dad's will," Brett sneered.

Adam nodded. "That's understandable. Who wants to be forced into . . . anything? Especially Morgan! What in hell possessed the old man to do such a crazy thing?"

Morgan unfolded her arms and, motioning, muttered sarcastically, "His lawyer advised him."

"Now, Morgan, I told you—"

Adam's keen sense for keeping peace motivated his interruption. "How about a drink? It's been a grueling day. Reading a will isn't exactly my idea of fun!"

Morgan flashed, "I'll drink to that! Make mine a double!"

Brett looked sharply at her. "Since when did you start drinking doubles, little sis?"

"Today! Since my own brother and my own dear departed daddy gave me the shaft!" She was near tears as she grabbed the small, old-fashioned glass Adam slid toward her and spilled a little of the pungent liquid over her hand. Perhaps she could get drunk and obliterate the events of this day from her weary mind.

Adam and Brett exchanged comments. Suddenly they were business partners with common interests, the men in the family —the decision-makers!

Meanwhile Morgan climbed onto a stool and leaned on the counter, attempting to assuage her anger with the glass of Scotch. It wasn't working, but it kept her busy. She had never felt so miserable in her life. How could her father do this to her? And she'd thought she was the apple of his eye. Ha! He must have hated her! After all, not only was there the crazy stipulation about her marrying, but the way the estate property was divided was decidedly unfair. Brett and Adam got the profitable land, the apartment buildings in Denver and Santa Fe. The business offices in Denver were also split between the brothers. Didn't he think she could manage business affairs? Even the gorgeous home Brett and his ritzy wife lived in was given to them.

And what did she get? The run-down ranch where they all

played cowboys as kids! Her father had bought it as a getaway place for his rambunctious family, providing room to roam. *Here's a chance to get back to nature,* he used to say. Hell, nobody had gotten back to nature down there in five years! Everyone was too busy. Brett had opened his new law office and Daddy had helped with that. Adam had been working his way through law school for years, it seemed. And she had been . . . well, maybe somewhat of a disappointment to her father. She had dropped out of college her senior year, opting for travel in Europe with friends. Persuading Daddy to finance the trip with her education money had been a real coup! She remembered the confrontation with the distinguished, gray-haired man.

"But, Daddy, this will be my education! Imagine going to the Louvre in Paris, London, Spain, Italy . . . Germany! Oh, Daddy! What could be a better education that that?"

He leaned back and puffed on an ebony pipe. "Yes, Morgana, it would be an education, of sorts. But it won't take the place of a college degree."

"Daddy, this is the chance of a lifetime! I just can't miss it! I won't!"

He puffed slowly, wondering how many times he'd heard those very statements from his energetic woman-child. His daughter had never wanted to miss a thing: she relished life's adventures. At least she knew what she wanted—and didn't want! Sighing, he acquiesced. "All right, Morgana. I never could oppose you. I'll arrange it with the bank tomorrow."

"Oh, Daddy, I love you!" She had hugged him quickly before dashing off. . . .

The drink sloshed against her lips and she licked it away, reluctant to lose a drop. Apparently the only way Brett Cassity, Sr., could oppose his beautiful, headstrong daughter was in death. And he had done it sufficiently. *Damn him!*

"Morgan! You'd better slow down on that drink! We'll be carrying you to your room if you keep that up!" Brett was acting very self-assured now that he was the leading male in the family and had received the first-born inheritance from his father. The fact that he was six years older than Morgana and four years Adam's senior had always given him the edge. Now—today— that gap seemed even larger to Morgan.

14

"Oh, shut up! Don't tell me what to do!" Morgan snapped.

"Hello, Morgana, darling. How are you doing now?" Brett's wife, Alise, breezed into the room, looking especially lovely and extremely happy for someone who had recently experienced a death in the family. Of course Brett, Sr., wasn't *her* family, not her blood relative, anyway. And by virtue of being married to Brett, Jr., she had come out on top of the estate heap. *Damn her, too!*

The world, it seemed, was against her. Morgan kept her back turned to Alise to avoid conversation.

"Hello, Alise," Brett said tightly. Anyone could tell the relationship between them was strained. Is that what Daddy wanted for her? Marriage, ha! Maybe Brett hadn't influenced their father, after all. He had denied wanting to force anyone into—

"Morgan isn't very happy, as you might understand."

"Well, it's been a difficult day." Alise's fluid voice slithered around the room. "I'll agree, Morgan. The will is unfair. You could contest it, you know. Shall we go, Brett? I'm tired."

"Sure, Alise." Brett returned his half-empty glass to the bar. "See you later, Adam. Morgan, cheer up. You'll feel better about this tomorrow. We'll work something out."

"Don't bother," muttered Morgan bitterly.

As the handsome couple left the room, Adam attempted to comfort his sister. "Morgan, I'm going skiing at Purgatory tomorrow. Why don't you go with me? I'm meeting an old friend. It'll be fun—a little relief from the strain of the last few weeks. This is probably the last snow of the season."

Morgan considered it for a moment, then demurred. "I don't feel like skiing, Adam. It sounds like too much fun," she muttered miserably, gazing into her rather blurry, empty glass. "Anyway, I have a job now. This is what Daddy's always wanted me to have. A job. And responsibility. Now I have both. And without a precious degree, too."

"What the hell are you talking about, Morgan?" Adam looked curiously at her, wondering if she was just drunk or completely out of her head.

"I'm going to turn that stupid ranch into a dude ranch and open for business the July fourth weekend. I'm going to settle down and be respectable. Maybe I can find myself a good ole cowboy to marry and have a dozen kids and spend my mornings cooking for the chuck wagon and my afternoons mending fences. Maybe that'll satisfy everyone."

"Morgan, you're talking crazy!"

"That's what Daddy wanted, isn't it?" Tears burned her eyes as the drink helped to reduce her anger to salty liquid.

Adam shook his head, and gentle brown eyes that matched hers revealed his sympathy. "No, I don't think that's what he had in mind. . . ."

"What, then?" Morgan implored.

Adam was at a loss for sufficient words to explain his father's rash rationale. "Well, I think maybe—"

"He wanted me to settle down!"

Adam sighed. There was no appeasing her. "Maybe so, Morgan. But actually I think your idea for a dude ranch is a good one. I read just the other day that the urban cowboy craze has influenced a current trend for dude ranching."

"Really?" She stared at him blankly.

"Oh, yes. Of course, July fourth is only three months away. That doesn't give us much time. . . ."

"Us?" she questioned, lifting her brown eyes to his.

"I'd like to help you get started. I don't take my bar exams until June, so I can't really be an official lawyer until after that. I had planned to work at Brett's office doing research. However I would enjoy working on the ranch, plus it would certainly provide the solitude I need to study for the bar. I want to help you, Morgan. Honest!"

Morgan's eyes narrowed as she answered in mocking tones. "Is that guilt creeping out? Feeling a little sorry for kid sister? Well, don't!"

He shrugged and grinned, determined not to let her set him on edge as she had Brett. After all she had a right to be upset. "A little guilt, maybe. Definitely not sympathy! You can do anything you set your little head to do, Morgan. Tell you what . . . I'll ski at Purgatory for a few days, then drive on over to the ranch at Vallecito. That'll give you time to pack and drive down. I'll meet you there!"

Morgan smiled up at Adam with tears glistening in her sad eyes. "Oh, Adam . . . thanks!" And as she hugged her brother's broad shoulders, the sharp memory of similar occasions with her father pierced her brave facade. . . .

The phone's abrupt ringing assaulted the soothing quiet, jangling loudly against the bare windowpanes and bouncing off the walls of the nearly empty rooms. Morgan's boots echoed as she walked hurriedly toward the newly installed instrument.

"Hello . . ." Her voice sounded strange after two days of relative silence in the old ranch house.

"Morgana?"

"Who else?" She recognized Brett's voice right away. What the hell did he want?

His voice was light. "Just checking on you. Have you heard from Adam?"

Instantly she was defensive. "Nope. He's due here today or tomorrow. And he's going to help me this summer, Brett. He offered and you agreed. Don't try to persuade him to return to Denver." It would be just like him to try to convince Adam that he was needed elsewhere, like in the law office.

There was a small pause and Morgan could hear Brett's sigh. "There's been a change of plans, honey."

Honey? Damn him! What does he want? "Brett! Don't do—"

"Listen to me, Morgan," Brett interrupted. "Adam's had a little accident. Nothing too serious, but it does alter your plans with him."

Morgan halted, heart pounding. "Little accident?" *What, now?*

Brett spoke quickly. "Adam broke his leg skiing. He's okay, just incapacitated with a full leg cast."

Morgan couldn't believe her ears. "Broke his leg? Skiing? Is he all right? Where is he?"

"He's in Durango's Mercy Hospital. I've talked to him and he's fine. Morgan, I want you to check him out of the hospital, since he was admitted overnight. I've arranged for an air ambulance to fly him back to Denver today. Will you go to the hospital and see that everything goes smoothly? I want him treated well. Can you do that?"

Morgan sighed. "Of course I can. But, Brett . . . what about the ranch? What—"

17

Brett's voice was abrupt. "Scratch it for now, honey. You can't do it alone."

Stunned, she answered, "I'll let you know when Adam's plane is due in Denver." As Morgan's hand replaced the receiver, her grip tightened until the knuckles were white with determination. Through thin lips she muttered, half aloud, "No, brother dear. I won't scratch it! I'll show you I can do it alone!"

Morgan's boot heels resounded in the hospital hall as she determinedly strode toward Adam's room. She pushed open the door and a slight gasp escaped her startled lips. She hadn't really considered her brother's appearance: that he might look different. Sitting in that stark-white hospital bed, he appeared so . . . oh, God! . . . *hurt* . . . with his leg stretched out and wrapped in that chalky cast. Even his usually tanned face was pale and drawn in pain.

"Adam! What in the devil did you do to yourself?" She crossed the room and kissed his forehead. It hurt her to see him in such a condition, and she completely forgot about their plans for the ranch.

Adam managed a tight chuckle. "What a way to end the skiing season. There just wasn't enough snow to cover all the rough spots. I should have known better! It was so quick, Morgan. One tip hit a rock and—wham! If it weren't for Grant here, I would probably still be out there on that slope. Nobody with any brains tackles the back side of Purgatory this time of year!"

Morgan winced as she listened to Adam's account. Finally she swung her gaze to the man who stood by the window and gave him a formulated smile. "Thanks for helping my crazy brother. I am so glad you were there!"

"Grant LeMaster," Adam offered, "meet my kid sister, Morgan Cassity."

The man's lips curled into a smile and his blue-gray eyes boldly assessed her. "I'm glad I was there, too, especially now that I get to meet his attractive sister. I guess Adam and I were both a little crazy yesterday. We knew from the ski reports that the snow was spotty. We just had to challenge the mountain one more time!" He laughed and shrugged his lean shoulders.

Morgan propped her fists on her slim hips. "And a fine price

18

you're paying, Adam, for the big challenge!" Her jeans were designer labels, her burgundy sweater velour, and she drew up to her full height of five feet, three inches . . . maybe four with the cowboy boots. It was the only time she'd ever been able to tower over her tall brother, and she relished every minute. "What would you have done if Grant hadn't saved you? My God, Adam, that's dangerous!"

Adam grinned sheepishly. "Save the lecture, Morgan. I'm lucky and I know it. Grant performed a regular Boy Scout act by dragging me two miles, and I'm no lightweight! It was a tough day for both of us."

Morgan turned to the stranger with renewed appreciation. "Well, Grant, that's quite a remarkable story. A simple thanks hardly seems enough." She was, for the first time, fully aware of the man outlined by the light from the window. He was tall and hard-muscled with a rugged, western appearance. The worn jeans, the soft chambray shirt, even the scruffy boots seemed to be a part of him, his look. Morgan delighted in the raw masculinity of the man, from his long, straight legs to his narrow hips, the squared span of his shoulders, the unkempt shadow along his jawline, the sprinkling of gray hair at his temples. He reminded her of the men in Europe, only his attire was different. But those steel-gray eyes . . . they smoldered with forbidden excitement. . . .

Morgan suddenly realized that she was staring open-mouthed at this stranger! She clamped her lips shut, then unable to resist, asked, "Don't I know you from somewhere?"

The tanned skin around his devilish eyes wrinkled with his laughter. "Hey, that's my line! I doubt if we've met. I think I'd remember you, Morgan."

She forgot they were standing in a hospital room, that Adam was watching this exchange between them. "Have you ever been to Europe?" The question dwindled at the end, for she knew the answer. Perhaps he was the type of man she had searched for all over Europe. Perhaps . . .

"Hey, remember me?" Adam jolted them both to the stark reality of the hospital room. "I thought you were going to spring me from this prison, Morgan!"

"Oh, I am, Adam. The, uh, plane should take off for Denver

19

in about an hour. I've already checked you out of the hospital, and we're just waiting for an ambulance to take you to the airport. Are you ready to go? Where are your things?"

He pointed to the disarrayed heap of clothes stuffed into a large plastic bag supplied by the hospital, and Morgan busied herself organizing them.

"Morgan." Adam's hand reached for hers. "I'm sorry about the ranch. Really, I am."

She flashed him a warm smile and shrugged off his concern. "Don't worry about that at all, Adam. I'll just hire some wrangler here in town to help me out." Her eyes settled immediately on the rugged cowboy appearance of Grant LeMaster and spontaneously asked, "Grant, you look like a pretty good cowboy. Could you use a job?"

Grant's gray eyes flickered briefly from Adam's to Morgan's, where they rested approvingly. "Well . . . yes, you could say that," he drawled.

Adam raised up on his elbow. "Morgan, this man's no more a cowboy than I am! He's a writer—"

Grant rocked back on his cowboy-boot heels and shrugged his angular shoulders. "I just do a little free-lancing. Right now, I'm—uh—between assignments, as they say. And I'm always looking for unusual jobs."

Morgan's confidence grew as she realized that he was indeed interested in working for her. "Well, I don't know how fascinated you'll be with my ranch, Grant, because it's going to be a hard job. It'll take a real man to work it."

A slow smile parted his insolent mouth, and Morgan noticed a slight indentation in his shadowy chin. "I think I qualify, but what a challenge!"

"Well, what I mean is . . ." Morgan stumbled over her words. "It's very hard work and . . . I don't know if you . . . I mean, a writer isn't exactly very physical . . . I need someone who can really work, not stand around and take notes!"

Grant folded his sinewy arms and flashed a quick grin at Adam. "Let's see now. You want someone who's a real man, who's physical, and who doesn't stand around taking notes. Tell you what, I promise not to take notes! The other, I guess I'll just have to prove! You're a tough boss, Morgan."

Adam howled with laughter. "My God, Morgan! This man's
—"

But he was interrupted by a firm hand on his shoulder and
Grant's affected drawl. "I'd be mighty pleased to help you at the
ranch, ma'am. And I'll try hard to be a real man." He paused
and Adam again hooted with laughter while Morgan burned
inside at their teasing. Then Grant added in a serious tone, "Only
trouble is, I'm not alone. I have a six-year-old son. Would you
be willing to take us both?"

"Sure. Why not? I can't pay you much, but it'll be a regular
salary, for a change. And of course you can have room and board
at the ranch." She didn't think that a child would create any
problems.

"Regular salary?" sputtered Adam. "Morgan—"

Again he was interrupted by Grant's determined voice. "Now,
Adam, don't worry about Morgan. I'll do my best to take good
care of your sister."

Adam chuckled and shook his head. He commented sarcastically, "I'm not worried about her, Grant. I'm concerned about
you!"

Grant's laugh came from low in his chest as he cast a confident
glance at Morgan's petite figure, then back to Adam. "I can
handle myself. You just take care of that broken leg and don't
worry about Morgan and me. We'll manage just fine."

"Of course, we will," agreed Morgan as a nurse and two
medics bustled into the room.

The nurse's ever-optimistic voice entoned, "Good afternoon,
Mr. Cassity. Are you ready to go home?"

Morgan and Grant stood by helplessly watching as Adam was
skillfully maneuvered onto a stretcher. Morgan clutched the
small duffel bag containing Adam's clothes and followed the
short caravan down the hall. Silently she wondered what Adam
would have done without Grant yesterday on that cold mountain. She shivered at the chilling thought and was filled with a
tremendous sense of gratitude—and a little intrigue—for Grant
LeMaster. She watched his ambling gait as he walked in front
of her and chatted briefly with the EMTs who had taken charge
of Adam. He might be a writer, but he looked as though he spent
more time being a cowboy. She could picture him astride a

quarter horse, cutting dogies and riding the range. And he probably whiled away his nights doing the cowboy two-step. She wouldn't object to dancing close to him . . . those broad, lean shoulders— What was she thinking? She had just hired the man! She had to retain some sort of supervisory distance between them, didn't she?

Morgan drove behind Adam's ambulance and Grant's burgundy Suburban to La Plata Airfield, outside of Durango. She noticed a child's head bobbing around in the vehicle with Grant, but paid little heed. At the airport she pulled to a stop next to the red and white ambulance, just as a slight child darted from the Suburban to a small Cessna plane parked nearby. Must be the son Grant referred to, she thought absently.

Grant diligently accompanied Morgan and Adam to the air ambulance, where a nurse and the pilot awaited their injured passenger. Morgan's apprehension grew as the nurse explained the various emergency equipment aboard. There was something about seeing her brother in the midst of IVs and oxygen masks and stethoscopes that was frightening. After trying to reassure Morgan that this kind of trip was very routine in the accident-prone ski area, the nurse smiled at Adam. "Well, are you ready to go?"

Morgan leaned over her brother's pale, drawn face. "Adam, you'll be home before you know it. And Brett will meet your plane when you arrive. I'll call him as soon as you take off." She tried to convey a positiveness that she really didn't feel.

Adam smiled wryly, apparently trying to cheer her, too. "Yeah, and he'll probably have the whole damn place snapping to attention."

Morgan smiled and patted his shoulder. "Yes, it'll undoubtedly beat the reception you got here. You know how Brett likes to get things done."

As she kissed his taut cheek, Adam murmured, "You've got yourself a real man, Morgan. Handle with care."

He shook hands with Grant, and within moments they had shoved Adam's stretcher inside, the doors were closed, and the plane began to taxi down the runway. As she watched the plane take off and rise rapidly to clear the mountains, a sob rose within Morgan. Aloud, she voiced her fears, seeking the reassurance

22

that Grant was only too glad to give. "Do you think he'll be all right? We don't even know them and he's so—"

Grant's voice was strong beside her. "Of course, Morgan. Adam's case is routine." His arm encircled her shoulders and he pressed her to him, repeating essentially what the nurse had just told them. "They do this all the time. You saw the equipment on board. It looked like a hospital. He'll be just fine."

Morosely she watched the plane disappear in the azure Colorado sky, and Adam's curious statement about Grant returned to her. Who was this man who stood so tall and reassuring beside her? Was it a mistake to hire him? After all, she knew absolutely nothing about him except that he was a friend of her brother's. What did Adam mean by "handle with care"?

She turned to face Grant, and his hand slid to rest lightly on her arm. For a long moment each looked into the other's eyes. He had touched her easily, naturally. And she had been receptive to his offering. Now she gazed closely into gray eyes that hinted of mystery. Tiny laugh lines fanned out from the corners onto tanned cheeks. His nose was straight and flanked by a crease on either cheek that led past his mouth. His squared jawline was covered with short, dark stubble where he had apparently not bothered to shave. Her eyes traveled back to his mouth where the lower lip protruded provokingly. Instinctively she swallowed, trying to eliminate the choking knot in her throat.

He broke the spell by squeezing her arm. "Morgan, come and meet my son." Then he moved a few steps away from her and called, "David! Come over here!"

In a moment the young boy stood before them, a slim, lithe child. His hair was jet black and he gazed soberly up at Morgan with the most beautiful ebony eyes she'd ever seen. Instantly she was reminded of the large-eyed Indian children painted by De Grazia, one of her favorite western artists.

Grant squatted down so that he would be eye level with the child. "David, this is Morgan Cassity. Morgan, meet my son, David."

Morgan extended her hand and he took it timidly. "It's nice to meet you, David." She smiled. This child was obviously of American Indian heritage. The traits must come from his mother, because Grant certainly didn't look . . .

23

Grant related the plan. "She is Adam's sister, David. And we are going to work on her ranch for a while. Would you like that?"

A distinct light crossed David's eyes as he acknowledged to Grant that the idea pleased him. Taking his son's hand, Grant stood. "Are you ready to go, Morgan? Why don't you lead the way?"

"Do you need to pack or get your things?"

He shrugged. "We live rather simply. Show us your ranch—we'll pick up our things later." He adjusted a handsome, dove-colored Stetson and led David toward the Suburban, talking and pointing at the planes that were parked nearby.

As Morgan watched them, she felt that there was something incongruous about that gorgeous hat. It was too . . . expensive. And so was the Suburban. But she shrugged and headed for her Camaro, grateful that at least she had found someone to help her now that Adam was unable.

Grant turned to her before reaching his vehicle. "Don't forget to call your brother in Denver about Adam. Just use the airport phone."

She nodded meekly. How could she have forgotten about Adam so soon? But she had.

Morgan's white Camaro headed over hills, into valleys, followed by Grant's large, burgundy, four-wheel-drive vehicle. They drove the twenty miles away from the small town of Durango, into the beautiful narrow valley where the ranch was located. The entire area backed up to the San Juan Wilderness and was a favorite of sportsmen and naturalists alike. As Morgan drove into the familiar rutted driveway, the place seemed suddenly very remote. And she was here alone with a stranger.

She crawled out of her compact car and watched the lean cowboy behind her alight easily from his sturdy vehicle while the boy ran over to a broken-down fence and proceeded to climb around. Grant ambled toward her, glancing curiously around him at the run-down ranch. Being all alone, the only sound they heard was wind rustling through giant ponderosa pines.

Apprehensively Morgan wondered what in hell she was doing. She had actually put herself in a very dubious position—out here so far from civilization with a perfect stranger. But surely Adam would have warned her if he thought she would be in danger. *No,* she tried to assure herself, *he's perfectly safe. Adam said it would be fine.* *"You've got yourself quite a man"* rang in her mind.

"You're going to turn this place into a dude ranch, Morgan? You've got a big job before you," Grant said, shaking his head dismally.

Morgan nodded solemnly. *"We,* Grant. We have a job before us. That's what you're hired for, remember? We have a dude ranch to put together before July fourth."

His dark brows arched. "July fourth? You're pushing it some, aren't you? I don't think we can get it ready by then."

She shrugged. "I've already advertised. And I have one family, friends from Denver, committed as customers. So we have to. Adam thought we could do it, if we work very hard. If you're not willing, now is the time to back out."

He pushed the cowboy hat back on his head with his thumb. "Well, if Adam could do it, that's good enough for me." He gazed at her steadily with gray, penetrating eyes. "I'm not a quitter. Especially before I've begun. We'll stay, Morgan. And we'll get the job done before July fourth, if that's what you want."

She smiled spontaneously, warmly responding to his avowal. "Great! That's what I wanted to hear. I think we can do it, too, Grant." She took a few steps up toward the high porch of the ranch house.

"I'm sure David is hungry by now. Where can we eat?" He took a step after her, but still had to look up to where she stood.

"You can fix yourselves sandwiches in the ranch-house kitchen. Sorry there isn't much food around here yet."

He propped a booted foot casually on the step above him and leaned an elbow on his knee. A little caustically he said, "One important thing you'll need here is lots of food. And you'd better get used to cooking a decent meal because when you have a hardworking crew of wranglers and a houseful of guests, a sandwich won't do."

Morgan's sable eyes hardened. "I'll hire a cook when that time comes, Grant. But will a sandwich do for tonight?"

"Sure, David and I are hardy. We can make it on anything." He ascended the stairs and suddenly was towering beside her.

25

"Incidentally," she directed tersely, "you'll sleep in the bunk-house. I'll get you some blankets. And breakfast will be at eight."

His directive was equally as terse. "You'd better make it at six. We have work to do. Anyway, you'll have to get used to the early hours."

"My, my! What would I do without my *hired hand* who informs me about all the things I'll have to do on my own ranch!" She turned away sharply and disappeared into the house, her straight, golden hair trailing midway down her back, like fine silk just waiting to be spun.

CHAPTER TWO

Fragrant whiffs of cooking bacon breezed over Morgan's sleeping form, filling the darkened room with delicious morning smells. She stirred, turned over, and buried her head deeper while her golden hair fanned on the pillow. Then something—maybe it was the aroma of coffee mingling with the bacon—brought her to full consciousness. She lay very still, determining where she was and just who would be creating such a delicious disturbance.

Sitting straight up in bed, she knew! Grant LeMaster! He was in the house! What was he doing in *her* house? She was up in a flash, grabbing her silken robe, dashing down the hall. The old house was a rambling ranch-style with three large bedrooms located in a separate wing that was isolated from the activity area. Morgan had set herself up in the enormous end bedroom that her parents had shared, so it was quite a jaunt down a long L-shaped hallway to the source of the curious activity that had awakened her.

"What are you doing in here?" Morgan demanded on approaching the brightly lit kitchen.

Grant LeMaster, hired hand turned cook, looked up from his skillet and smiled warmly. "Morning! Coffee's ready. And breakfast will be in a few minutes."

Morgan propped her fists on her hips, forgetting to hold the robe together, so that her shapely legs were quite visible beneath the very short nightie. "Just what in hell are you doing?" She gulped and could have bitten her own tongue as large dark eyes peered at her from behind Grant. *The kid!* She had forgotten him! And there he was—awake as an owl!

Grant smiled indolently. "Well, David is working on cinnamon toast and I'm doing the bacon. How do you like your eggs?"

"Eggs?" Morgan blanched at the thought. She pushed the robe around her and quickly knotted the loose belt. Closing in on him, she muttered through clinched teeth. "What are you doing in my house? At this hour of the morning? And fixing all this . . . food!"

He gazed down arrogantly at her. "I told you six o'clock. We're late already. There's a full day's work to do, Morgan. I suggest you start with a cup of coffee." He nodded toward the busily perking pot.

Exasperated by the niggling thought that he was probably right, she moved numbly toward the pot, filled a mug, and slumped at the table. "Now that I'm awake, I may as well stay up. My God, what an hour! It's profane to rise before the sun. And to be so cheery about it."

"Oh, the sun's up. Has been awhile. You'll have to set your alarm if you can't get up naturally at this time."

"Naturally? This is the most unnatural thing I've ever done! Who ever gets up *naturally* at this hour?" She glowered sleepily into the face of the small boy who had approached her silently.

"I do," David said quietly. "Would you like some toast?" He held a platter of bubbly brown toast.

She looked closely into those dark, somber eyes and was struck by the depth of emotion they revealed. There was no reflection of herself; only his own sensitivity was apparent as he stared steadily at her.

"I . . . why, yes, David. It looks delicious." She reached humbly for one of the pieces of toast with their marvelously rich topping. "Where did you learn to make such great cinnamon toast?" She nibbled a bite, just for David's sake, and found it delicious.

Solemnly the child nodded to the tall man who beamed at him with pride. "From Grant." David put the platter of toast in the center of the table and sat quietly munching a taste of his own fare.

"Grant?" She arched her eyebrows at the man. "Well, isn't *Grant* clever!"

The man smiled satirically as he set heaping plates of bacon and eggs before her and David. "I try."

In a low voice she muttered, "Whatever became of *Dad,* or *Papa*?"

He lowered himself into the chair next to her. "David and I have a very friendly relationship. We're pals, aren't we, partner?" He tousled David's straight black hair affectionately.

"If you're his pal, who's his father?" She couldn't seem to avoid her tartness this morning.

Grant turned his steel-cold gaze on her. "Look, I'll handle the management of my son. You take care of your business at the ranch. So far you haven't done so hot at your job, so don't tell me how to do mine!"

"How the he—" She stopped abruptly, remembering the child across the table from her. Evenly she tried again. "How can I, when you enter *my* home and start your business in *my* kitchen before I'm even out of bed?"

"Well, someone had to do it! I expected food on the table at six. We have a full day ahead, so eat up." He motioned to the pile of scrambled eggs on her plate.

"You expected—" She glared at Grant, then caught sight of large eyes set in a small dark face watching for her reaction. She forced her lips into a tight smile, picked up the fork, and began pushing the egg around for just the right tiny bite.

Silence hung heavily in the air while Grant and David finished off the entire plate of cinnamon toast, and Morgan struggled with each minuscule bite she took. Breakfast at six! How awful! And all this food! She remembered the marvelous croissants and coffee in the little French cafés. There, they slept as late as they wanted. And the doughnuts . . . and the little German bakery shops where they rode their bikes to savor the marvelous delicacies before choosing the perfect thick sweet rolls and an extra bag of shortbreads. Oh, that was nice. . . .

A voice jolted her back to the six o'clock breakfast and Grant LeMaster. ". . . and while I'm making a quick assessment of the

29

buildings, you begin making a list of supplies. Start with meat and potatoes. I'll be back shortly and we'll tour the property. We need to know the condition of the trails and just how far the ranch goes. Later we'll go into town for supplies. We can't do a thing without equipment and supplies."

Morgan stared numbly at Grant as he left his plate in the sink. How dare he issue orders to her like that? Just whose ranch is this anyway?

"And you might clean up this kitchen while you're thinking about supplies." As David headed out the door, Grant stopped beside her. In a low breath he said, "And get dressed. I don't know how many mornings I can endure staring at those bare-faced nipples over coffee."

Morgan came to life as she hopped to her feet. "Bare—! Well, we'll take care of that problem right now! You get out of my house! How dare you say that to me! I think one of the first things on the supply list will be a hot plate so you and David can cook your own breakfast out there and leave me alone!" She motioned toward the bunkhouse with a slim hand, which Grant immediately enclosed between his palms.

The sensuous warmth from his hands pulsed through her as his velvet voice permeated the air. "Now, now, hold your temper. We have a certain image to uphold for little David," he admonished sarcastically.

Her voice was shrill. "I don't give a damn about image! And I don't intend to face you over breakfast every day at six! You can fix your own meals and stay out of my house!" She pulled her hand from his and tucked it securely under her other arm. Damn him, anyway! He had her perspiring at this hour!

His lips moved close to her face, showing his white, even teeth as he spoke. "We're wasting time, you know. It's nearly seven. I have work to do and you have . . . enough to keep you busy. I'll be back in an hour. Be ready." He turned his broad back on her and strode out.

There was something so smug and authoritarian and . . . commanding about him that infuriated Morgan. Worse yet, he was undoubtedly right! She stared at the closed door for a few moments, stifling the urge to sling her coffee cup after him. Instead she refilled it and stomped angrily to her room. Getting

30

dressed was her first priority. After what he'd said to her, she didn't dare appear until she was completely decked out.

She tugged on her designer jeans and pulled a chocolate brown sweater over her head against the chill of the April morning. Damn Grant LeMaster! What had Adam said about him? Quite a man? What could Adam possibly have seen of value in the man? Maybe he didn't know Grant very well. Maybe Grant just picked him up on the ski slope! Oh, dear God! Could it be that he was a total stranger to them all? She made a mental note to contact Adam immediately . . . at least, as soon as normal people woke up! Whatever had drawn her to this man's sex appeal in the first place? He was attractive, in a rough-hewn sort of way. But she was wrong to compare him with the European men. He was nothing like them. There wasn't a polite bone in his body. He was an arrogant bas—

The ringing of the phone blasted into her angry thoughts. Almost spastically she reached for it, wondering who could be calling her so early.

"Morgan, did I get you up?"

"Brett! What do you want at this hour?" Suddenly a sinking fear hit her. *What's wrong now?* So much had happened lately, she was getting paranoid.

"Aw, your warmth is showing, Morgan. Just thought I'd check on you before I go to work. And I wanted you to know that Adam arrived safely."

"Mostly to check on me, I suppose," Morgan snapped.

"You might say I'm concerned about you. Matter of fact, I don't think it's a good idea for you to stay at that ranch by yourself. I want you to come on back to Denver. In only six weeks or so Adam will be able to help you. By then maybe all of us can come down for a few weekends and help you get the place in order. You'll just have to wait a few weeks to get started."

"Come back to Denver?" Slowly she seethed inside. "Brett, I don't have to stop my life just because Adam broke his leg. I have a job to do here, remember?"

"Morgan, it's too dangerous for you to be there alone."

"I'm not alone. I've hired a . . . a cowboy, a wrangler," she spouted proudly. She wouldn't tell Brett what a jackass he was!

31

Brett's chuckle infuriated her. "Yeah, well, Adam and I have discussed that. And we've agreed that you can't manage it alone. And that dude's no cowboy. He's a writer and knows nothing about ranching . . . dude or otherwise."

Suddenly she was defending him. "He certainly does! Why, we're assessing the property today and going in for supplies later. I'm busy, Brett. And I'm not closing up here to return to Denver until you and Adam determine when I can go to work."

"Morgan, you're impossible. And goddamn stubborn!"

"It's a family trait, brother dear," she grated into the phone. "Gotta go. I have a ranch to run. Thanks for your concern." With a snap she hung up the phone. How dare he tell her what to do! She'd be damned if her brothers would manage her life! She'd run this ranch or die trying! She was still shaking with anger when a scraping noise, like a heel on the bare floor, attracted her attention. Whirling, she encountered the chiseled face of Grant LeMaster standing in the doorway to her bedroom!

"What are you doing here?" she demanded.

He folded his arms and looked at her. "Seems I've already heard that question this morning. I see you haven't cleaned up the kitchen. Do you have your supply list made?"

"And I'm getting tired of asking the same questions over and over! What are you doing in my bedroom?" she sputtered again.

His smile was mocking and those gray eyes raked over her. "I thought you could use some help."

"Well, I think I can manage to dress myself! Now you get out of here!" Why wouldn't they leave her alone? All of them! And why had she defended this arrogant, brazen man to her brother? Morgan knew nothing about him, except that he put her on edge . . . and that his eyes were daringly gray. Defiantly she exposed what she did know about him. "I understand that you're not a cowboy, after all. Why did you pretend you were?"

"I didn't. You jumped to that conclusion. However I'm not a complete stranger to horses. Even tried my hand at rodeoing. I came along for the creative experience."

"Creative experience? What the hell do you mean by that?" She felt more manipulated by the minute.

"Just a fancy way of getting experience that I might be able to incorporate into my writing sometime."

32

"You're going to write about this? My ranch? *Me?* Oh, no you don't! You may as well hit the road now. I need someone who can work, not write!"

"I told you I could handle the job. And I intend to. Anyway, I told Adam I'd look after you. I can't go back on my word, now, can I? Not with him laid up with a broken leg. Now, if you'll get your boots on, we can be on our way. I'll be doing your job in the kitchen while I'm waiting for you, Morgan." He turned on his heel and left her fuming.

"My job is *not* in the kitchen!" she yelled at his receding back. Grabbing the fancy cowboy boots, she tugged them on and stuffed her jeans down into them. Furiously she brushed her silken hair to a shine then braided it quickly, letting it drape over one shoulder. A little lip gloss was the only makeup she bothered with today. After all, whom would she see? Only Grant LeMaster.

First Grant insisted that she accompany him through the outbuildings of the ranch. Dismissing the earlier sharp words, they somehow managed to discuss the pros and cons of which buildings would be needed for immediate use, which needed only painting, which needed remodeling.

Little David hopped, ran, and hid in the empty rooms, staying close but not underfoot. He was a quiet, undemanding child and Morgan found that she didn't mind having him around at all. It was his father that disturbed her.

Then they toured the far reaches of the ranch in Grant's Suburban. The four-wheel-drive vehicle was well suited to the rough roads that plunged through the rugged terrain, and Morgan was grateful for it. She was sure her Camaro couldn't have made it. As they drove along, she pointed out landmarks of the property and Grant dictated items for her to jot down on the supply list. Polite but terse conversation was kept to a minimum. After all this was business.

Following a brief lunch, which they all chipped in to prepare, the three of them set off for town. They spent some time in the hardware store, choosing the tools Grant thought he would need. Then he asked Morgan to do the groceries alone.

"I'll be back in an hour to pick you up, Morgan. David and

I will just pack up a few items from our apartment. See you soon."

"Okay. Can you think of anything else you'd like to have? What about you, David?" She smiled at the boy, whose ebony eyes gazed steadily at her.

He shrugged without a sound.

"What about doughnuts? And Cheerios? Every kid likes those."

His dark eyes traveled questioningly to Grant, who nodded with a wink. "Yes. I'd like that," he told her unemotionally.

She had never seen a more placid child. He didn't even get excited about doughnuts.

"And plenty of fresh fruit and vegetables. Growing boy, you know. And we've gotta take care of those good teeth," Grant added.

She glanced at him. "Spoken like an earnest father."

"Thank you, ma'am. Nicest thing you've said to me all day," he quipped. "Maybe there's hope for us yet, Morgan."

"I doubt it," she said as she opened the door. "If you just do the job I need, I'll be happy."

Grant nodded briskly. "That should be easy enough, because I'm going to do the job. Together, we'll make it." His steely gray eyes reassured her, and she crawled out of the large vehicle believing him.

Morgan glanced at the presumptuous father and unassuming son as they drove away, knowing that when they brought their belongings to the ranch, it clinched their staying more firmly. Is that what she wanted? Could she work with Grant LeMaster? He'd promised to do the job she needed. But what she really needed was a husband. Oh, God—what made her think of that just now? She clutched the grocery list and headed into the supermarket.

By nightfall Morgan slipped gratefully into bed. Supplies and tools had been bought and stored in appropriate places, ready for the busy ranch life ahead. Dinner had been such an obstacle for Morgan that Grant and little David had prepared the pork chops and mashed potatoes, while Morgan was relegated to the salad. Few words were spoken as the three sat at the table together to eat . . . again. Grant had not gotten the threatened hot plate

34

along with the other necessary supplies today. So Morgan knew they would face each other again over the table in the morning. What an event to anticipate . . . with dread!

Finally Grant and David had moved into the bunkhouse, symbolizing to Morgan their intent to stay. She would have to face Grant LeMaster every morning, whether she wanted to or not. However there was some security in having him here. He would help her realize her goal. He had assured her of that.

Morgan gazed through the window as David struggled with a small suitcase and a large box of toys. Actually it wasn't very much for a child. But Grant had brought even less—two suitcases, one of which was square and could be a portable typewriter case. If so, he apparently had only one suitcase of clothes. He needed a job more than she realized. The move was quickly accomplished, the bunkhouse door closed, and the father and son were in to stay.

If Morgan thought she was tired that first night, it was nothing compared with how she felt by the end of the week. Each day began at six, despite her protestations, and ended, gratefully, at dusk. Then there was the evening meal to contend with. Most of the time Grant assisted, directing all of Morgan's efforts. And that was fine with her. She had no desire to take over the kitchen duties. Even little David seemed more comfortable in the kitchen than Morgan and more willing to do chores that needed to be done.

Morgan often watched the little boy in amazement. She had never seen such an agreeable child. Grant must be doing something right as a father, she thought, shaking her head, even if he did allow his son to call him by his first name.

By Saturday, Morgan was stiff and sore from the physical labor she had done all week. The muscles she used were totally different from the ones needed for a tennis match or day of leisurely swimming. At dusk she trudged toward the front stairs and sat wearily on the top step. Grant joined her, removing his straw working hat and wiping perspiration from his brow with his shirt sleeve. No words were necessary, for both were too exhausted to converse. They just watched David's energetic playing in the evening shadows.

35

Finally Morgan commented, "I don't know where he gets the energy to continue. He never seems to run down."

Grant smiled at the young boy, who played a game of hopping and tossing a small stone. "One thing's for sure. He sleeps well at night. I must admit, Morgan, he has really enjoyed being on the ranch this week. It seems to be a good place for him, and I'm glad you agreed to let him come. Not everyone would do that."

"He's a delightful child, Grant. In fact, he's about the quietest kid I've ever met. And he's very beautiful . . . or should I say, handsome," Morgan said sincerely.

"Yes, he is," agreed Grant, honestly.

"I suppose he looks like his mother . . ." Morgan began hesitantly. She couldn't help wondering about the child's mother . . . Grant's wife.

But Grant just nodded and grunted, "Uh-huh." He'd never offered any information about their lives, or why David was living with him instead of his wife . . . or former wife. The situation must be severe. What judge in his right mind would award a child to a father who had such an unstable life-style? Perhaps David's mother was dead?

Abruptly Grant changed the subject. "Do you have any plans for supper?"

She grinned and shrugged. "You know me. We'll whip something together, as usual."

"Why don't we go into town for a pizza tonight?" he suggested. "It's been a rough week and that would be a good treat for all of us!"

Morgan shook her head tiredly. "All the way into town for a pizza? It's so far and I'm so tired, Grant," she groaned.

"Well, I would suggest take-out service, but I don't think they'd deliver," he said wryly. "Come on, Morgan."

She looked into his smiling, tired eyes. "Do you really mean it? You'd drive all the way into town for a pizza?"

"Only if you'll go, too. Tell you what. You take a nice, warm bath and relax a little. David and I will shower and meet you in an hour. Then we can make our little jaunt into town together. It'll be fun."

"You're serious, aren't you?" She stifled a yawn. "I'm afraid if I get in the tub, I won't be able to get out again."

36

"Then I'll come and get you." He smiled and touched her nose. "If you don't want my help, meet us here in an hour." Turning, he started toward the bunkhouse. "Come on, David! Race you to the shower! We're going to town for pizza!" Grant suddenly exhibited a spurt of energy and ran laughing with his son across the yard.

Morgan sat in the dark for a few minutes, listening to the happy sounds of father and son before hurrying inside. If she could believe him—and she certainly did—she had better get her own bath and dress herself. Tonight she was going out, even if it was only with Grant LeMaster and his son.

Within the hour the three of them took off for town in high spirits. Grant drove the Camaro this time and David delighted in riding in the small car. To him everything was an adventure— it was a pleasure to watch him. The child's innocent joy was contagious, and soon Grant and Morgan abandoned their constant digging remarks. Pleasure was imminent, in spite of the stubborn characters involved. Was it possible that they could converse civilly? Enjoy an evening in harmony? Be polite to one another? Even go so far as to joke and laugh . . . together? It was happening . . . and they were led by a child.

Grant scanned the menu, then solicited opinions. "How hungry are you tonight? Should we share a large pizza?"

"Oh, yes! I'm starved!" agreed Morgan enthusiastically. "I'll have black olives, pepperoni, and anchovies, please." She glanced idly around the semidark pizza parlor. The decor reminded her of an old western saloon with low-hanging lamps over round tables and a makeshift bar along one wall. The only modern concession was the line of electronic games in the back.

"I want just sausage," David's small voice chimed in. "No peppers or 'chovies and *no* onions on mine!"

"Olives, not onions," Morgan corrected. "You'll like olives."

"No, I won't! I don't like olives or onions! Blah!"

Grant spread his hands. "Okay, okay! Let's start again. Could you two compromise, please? Morgan, I must admit, even I don't like anchovies."

She glared at him. "Can't we split it up—half and half?"

He leaned toward her with a twinkle in his eyes. "How would you suggest doing that? Half for you and the other half for David

37

and me? Can you eat that much?" He glanced up at the patiently waiting attendant. "I'm sorry. Why don't you take the next order while we discuss this?"

"Can't you make a decision, Grant?"

"Oh, I can. But trying to please you two is impossible! What about drinks?"

"Coke!" David cried.

"Root beer!" Morgan voted, laughing.

"Morgan, how about a Coors?" Grant said in mock exasperation.

"That'll be fine." Morgan snapped her fingers. "Tell you what, Grant. Hurry up and order whatever you feel David will eat. I'll concede. It doesn't matter to me. What David and I really want to do is play Pac-Man!"

"What's Pac-Man?" David looked up at her curiously.

"What's Pac-Man! Where have you been keeping this child, Grant? Come on, David. I'll show you! You make the big decision and order for us, Grant. We have confidence in you." She and David sorted through her purse for quarters. As they started toward the electronic games, she heard Grant ordering.

"We'll have three separate pizzas. One with anchovies, pepperoni, and black olives, one with just sausage, and the other . . ."

Soon he joined Morgan and David, watching in amazement at David's dexterity in maneuvering the little electronic gobbler. They took turns, but the small boy proved his skills to be sharper than either of the adult's. Totally absorbed in watching Grant's game, Morgan rested her hands casually on his angular shoulders, rooting for the round gobbling blob. It was only when the game was over that she realized she was brushing against him so easily.

Grant rose and draped a long arm around both her and David. "Our pizza's getting cold! Let's leave Pac-Man for another time."

Morgan smiled up at Grant, feeling slightly warmed by his closeness. She tried to pretend that his sudden familiarity didn't matter to her. But she knew better. His touch set her on fire.

Morgan insisted on buying an ice cream cone for David before leaving town.

38

"Yes, yes!" agreed David, showing definite enthusiasm.

Grant nodded to the west. "Swenson's is just down the street. I have an errand to run, so I'll meet you there in a few minutes."

"Okay," Morgan agreed, taking David's hand.

"What kind of ice cream do you want, Grant?" the boy asked his father.

Grant shook his head. "Oh, I don't want any ice cream, son. You go with Morgan and enjoy it." He didn't notice the expression of disappointment on David's face.

But Morgan did. "I can't decide between Peanut Butter Fudge and Cherry Cheesecake, David! How about you?"

He looked up at her with renewed interest. "I like Bubble Gum," he admitted, smiling.

Morgan returned the smile, and they started down the street hand-in-hand. They were finishing off their sugar cones when Grant drove up and honked.

As they climbed into the small car, David smiled cheerfully at Grant. "You missed the most fun, Grant! Morgan let me taste her ice cream and I let her taste mine! Next time we're going to try different kinds!"

Grant smiled at David, "Great, son." Then to Morgan he raised dark eyebrows. "Next time?"

"Sure." She nodded, a twinkle in her deep brown eyes. "We have twenty-nine other flavors to try!"

With a knowing gaze he uttered triumphantly, "For someone who didn't want to come in the first place, you certainly ended up having a good time."

"Yes." She smiled, ignoring his gloating attitude. "David and I had a great time."

As they drove home in the dark, they sang along with the radio until they realized that there were only two off-key voices. David had drifted off to sleep, curled up in the backseat. As they pulled into the driveway, Morgan placed her hand gently on Grant's arm. "This was a good idea, Grant. Thanks for making me go."

"I'm glad you went, Morgan, but I have the distinct feeling that no one could make you do anything you didn't want to." He paused and reached for a paper bag under his seat.

Morgan's breath caught in her throat at his statement, for she knew how wrong it was. Her father would make her do something she didn't want to do—marry!

"Here's an even better idea," Grant directed, handing her the brown bag. "Here. You get the glasses filled and I'll join you as soon as I tuck David in bed."

She looked at the telltale shape of the item he gave her and giggled. "You're full of great ideas tonight, cowboy!"

He was gone before Morgan had time to change her mind or to decide if this was the proper behavior for a boss-employee relationship. A glass of wine certainly sounded great right now. It had been a long, hard week, and they deserved a little relaxation.

By the time Grant arrived, Morgan was trying to light a fire in the fireplace. The wineglasses were filled and the remaining wine was in the refrigerator being chilled.

"Here, let me." Grant took over the fire-making chore, as he had taken over so many jobs around the place. Soon a friendly fire was licking around the logs. He settled heavily at the other end of the sofa from Morgan. Before saying a word, he drank several sips of wine and leaned his head against the back of his seat. His eyes were closed for several minutes and Morgan noticed that tired lines of fatigue were visible on his still countenance.

She tried to turn away from Grant's powerful, if tired, profile and concentrated instead on the growing fire. She sipped her wine but, despite its relaxing effect, she still felt his energy in the room. Finally she asked quietly, "Did David go back to sleep?"

Grant answered without even opening his eyes. "He didn't wake up. I undressed him and hauled him to bed, and he still didn't move. He's exhausted, but I think he really loves the ranch life, Morgan."

"Well, can you blame him? I suppose he's been cooped up in an apartment with you. This gives him room to roam."

"Yes. And he's missed that."

"Missed it? Did you have a ranch before . . ." She halted. *Before what?*

Grant opened his eyes and reached for his wineglass. "David's been with his grandmother. He hasn't lived with me very long."

Morgan couldn't retain her curiosity. "Where is his mother?"

He took another huge gulp of wine. "She's dead."

Morgan swallowed hard. So the mother was dead and the grandmother had cared for this child. Finally Grant had decided to take care of his own child.

"How long ago?" she asked gently.

"She died in childbirth."

In childbirth? Did that happen nowadays? Morgan thought in horror. How awful! To lose your wife and be left with an infant, all at once. "Grant, I'm so sorry. It must have been hard. But you have done a remarkable job. He is a terrific kid. I mean that sincerely."

He looked at her, puzzlement in his soft gray eyes. He studied her for a moment before answering. "His grandmother did that. But I agree, he is a pretty neat kid. And you should see him ski. He skied Bull Run at Purgatory with Adam and me the day Adam fell. That's a black slope, the most difficult. He even helped me move Adam. Yes, he's a special kid."

"I can tell you're proud of him," Morgan smiled.

Grant chuckled. "I guess I'm bragging too much, aren't I? But I'm really like a new father."

"How long have you had David?"

"Two months. Adam has been helping me with some legalities. You know, everything is complicated these days. That's why we met at Tamarron. The skiing was just a diversion."

"How did you meet Adam? I've never heard him mention you, Grant."

Grant laced his fingers behind his head and leaned back on them. "Adam and I met in college in an investigative journalism class—we had an assignment together. I don't know why he took that damn course. Maybe he wanted to know how investigative reporters think so he could defend against them someday."

"Grant!"

He sighed heavily. "Face the facts, baby. The legal system is just a game, too, you know. Anyway, after that we became drinking buddies. But he went on to law school and I went on to . . . whatever I've been doing. The only time we can get together is an occasional skiing trip."

She raised her eyebrows. "I'm surprised you went to college with Adam. You look—"

"Older?"

She laughed good-naturedly. "Frankly, yes."

He moved his hands, leaving one arm relaxed across the back of the sofa. "I am. Thirty and counting. I spent my young and sensitive years in Nam. That's why I have these gray hairs." He laughed and ran long fingers through the gray strands at his temples.

In an action beyond her control Morgan reached out with one hand and ran her fingers through his hair, too. "Was it bad?" she asked softly.

His chuckle was a sarcastic grunt. "Yeah. It was . . . horrible. Sometimes I—" His hand closed over hers and held it against his cheek, then slid it to his lips, where he kissed her palm. His eyes were closed, and he seemed to revel in the softness of her hand on his face. It was like electricity searing through her arm and body until she finally pulled away from his fiery touch.

He took a quick breath and adroitly changed the subject. "What about you, Morgan? What were you doing before you became a rancher?"

After his revelation of years spent in Vietnam, Morgan was almost ashamed to tell him she had frolicked away the last few years. "I . . . I went to college at the University of Colorado."

"Your major?" Obviously he was looking for something they had in common.

She paused, fearing they had absolutely nothing. "Liberal arts. But I didn't graduate. I . . . quit to go to Europe with friends." Why did she feel guilty about that? At the time, she thought it was a great idea.

"Europe? Wonderful! Where did you go? I've always wanted to see Europe. Tell me about it."

His enthusiasm dispelled any feelings of chagrin she had about the overseas trip. They talked late into the night as he eagerly questioned her about her trip to Europe and she regaled him with tales of her adventures and impressions. The bottle of wine was empty and the fire had burned to glowing embers before they realized it.

"My God, Morgan, it's late. I've got to go."

They both stood at the same time, eyes meeting in an unspoken surge of emotional attraction. The fragile bond between them had definitely been strengthened tonight by the fun and laughter, the wine and conversation.

Morgan smiled. There was a catch in her voice as she tried to convey her feelings. "Thanks for insisting that we go out tonight, Grant. It was . . . wonderful. And so was the wine."

"I enjoyed it, too, Morgan." His voice was low and apologetic. "I'm sorry that I've been a little rough on you this week. But there's just so much to be done around this place, and if you want to get it done by July . . ."

She shrugged, her deep brown eyes captivating him thoroughly. "I understand. I need someone like you, Grant. You've already been a great help. . . ." Her words dwindled at the end, as his hand cupped her face and turned it up to meet his feathery light kiss. "Don't go, Grant . . ." she breathed against the sensuous curve of his lips. Tonight he was more than the man she had hired—he was that mysterious stranger she had first met . . . and more. Much more. She trembled inside at the touch of his mouth against hers, but did not shy away from it.

He kissed her again, lightly. "I don't want to . . ." They stood close, still not touching except for his hand capturing her face, their eyes locked in tormented disquiet. She could hear his steady breathing and wondered if her own stifling gasp was obvious.

She choked out the words. "Stay for the summer . . ." Morgan closed her eyes for another kindling of lips and passion and braced herself for it by placing her hands on his waist. Her fingers gripped the worn leather belt that hugged his lean hips. She could feel the warmth radiating from his body and the quivering of rock-hard muscles as her hands grazed his broad back. Drawn to his unleashed power, she swayed into him and nestled her head into his chest, breathing in the delicious smell of his warmth.

His voice was hoarse. "I'll stay as long as you need me." With gratitude in her eyes she looked up at him and he bent down to her as if to drink in her liquid gaze. His lips covered hers in a demanding, fiery kiss. He gently caressed her back, moving his hands in enticing strokes, finally settling on the soft curves of her breasts. Soft gasps escaped from deep in her throat as he feathered light satiny kisses along her smooth neck. His strong arms engulfed Morgan, pulling her completely to him, molding her to his trembling body. His tongue again teased her lips apart to taste her sweet mouth, sending a torrent of hot passion coursing through her body. The moments hung like eternity as she was lost in the ecstasy of Grant's arms, his kiss, his overwhelming magnetism. Morgan did not pause to wonder why she was drawn to the strength of this man she barely knew. But she melted inside with the unmistakable pleasure of his touch. And she never wanted it to end.

Morgan's arms reached up to the strength of his shoulders, clinging, pulling him down to her. There was no escaping his demanding mouth, his encompassing arms, his unyielding passion, his steel-gray eyes. Slowly she realized she hadn't pulled him down to her at all. He had effortlessly lifted her off her feet to meet his searing kiss! He held her firmly with one arm around her back and the other grasping the soft curve of her buttocks. She moaned as her breasts were crushed against the firm muscles of his chest and her nipples hardened at the pleasurable friction. Lost in the ever-mounting sensations, she gently traced her tongue along the outline of his ear with quick, flicking strokes. Grant groaned, sinking both his hands into the soft flesh of her buttocks, pulling her closer to his ever-increasing desire. He opened his mouth against her moist lips, easing his tongue across the ridge of her teeth, possessing her tongue with his own.

Morgan unclasped her arms from behind his neck with a shudder, and pushed on his shoulders with a determined sigh. This had to stop; they both had responded too eagerly to what began as a casual kiss! Her feet dangled helplessly as she awaited Grant's response to her withdrawal.

He lifted his passion-darkened face from hers and whispered hoarsely, "Morgan, I . . . have to . . . go. Or I'll never stop." Releasing his hold on her, he allowed her to slide down the long length of his chest and thighs.

As her feet touched the floor, she clutched at his arms momentarily, steadying herself. "Grant, I . . . this can't go on . . ." She dropped her arms to her sides, feeling weak and shaken.

He shook his head and ran his long fingers through his dark, unruly hair. "You're right, Morgan. We have to work together." Her eyes were pleading. "It . . . it won't happen again, Grant."

44

It can't. But . . . please say you'll stay the summer. I . . . need you." *Oh, God, I want you!*

He nodded mutely, not daring to speak or touch her again. If only she knew how badly he needed—desired—her, she would send him packing tonight!

As if she could read his mind through those smoldering gray eyes, Morgan whispered, "You'd better go now, Grant." She smiled faintly, suddenly feeling shy before the tall man who had kissed her so thoroughly, literally sweeping her off her feet.

Without a word he turned around and was gone. Weakly Morgan sank onto the sofa, staring into the glowing embers in the otherwise dark fireplace. *Oh, dear God, what's happening to me? Am I so gullible, so vulnerable that I can't resist this man? Or am I falling in love . . . again?*

CHAPTER THREE

The sun, streaming brilliantly over Morgan's bed, finally aroused her. Or was it the wonderful aroma of perked coffee? She stretched lazily, arching her stiff back and flexing sore, shapely leg muscles. Yes, there was definitely coffee brewing somewhere in the house, and she knew she had to have some. With a great deal of effort Morgan rolled out of bed and clutched the blue silken robe around her. She shuddered involuntarily as she splashed ice-cold water on her face, trying to wash away the wrenching effects of the late-night wine she and Grant had shared. What she really needed was to brush her teeth and drink about a gallon of coffee. *Oh, damn! Why did I do that last night?* But, deep inside, she knew. She knew, but wouldn't admit it, didn't dare think it.

She stumbled out to the massive den, where Grant was intently concentrating on writing. Dear God, he was handsome as he sat with his bare feet propped up, long legs stretched out, dark head bent over his work. His long arm reached absently for his cup of coffee, bringing it to his lips for a long gulp. *Those lips!* Morgan tingled as she recalled the provoking disorder his sensuous lips had created within her. *Oh, no!* What in the world was she thinking? She was the boss around here and wouldn't allow *that* to happen again! They had both agreed to it! She shook off the mixed feelings, cleared her throat, and quickly headed to the kitchen and much-needed coffee.

Finally, completely recovered, she joined Grant, steaming cup in her hand. Before she had a chance to speak, he smiled and remarked cheerfully, "Good morning, beautiful. How are you this morning?"

She eyed him narrowly. "How can you be so chipper? And why are you up so early?"

He chuckled. "Aw, did the wine bother you? Feeling a little thick-headed?"

She didn't like his choice of words and turned her back on him, staring blankly out the window. "No. I just can't stand people who are so damned cheery in the morning."

"Well, somebody's got to present a pleasant face to David. And what good is a grump?"

Her comment was short. "You're the father."

"And I thank God for that kid every day! I'll do whatever is necessary to keep him, too! I don't give a damn if I have to get up at the crack of dawn every day! If you don't like it, we'll leave now!" The words exploded from the previously placid form of Grant LeMaster, echoing the fervor of his convictions through the nearly empty ranch house.

Morgan blanched beneath his barrage of angry words. "Grant, I . . ." she attempted weakly, turning to him. "I didn't mean to offend you. I know how much you care for David. And I certainly wasn't hinting that you . . . you two . . . leave. I'm sorry. I shouldn't have said that."

He sighed and ran his hand over his face. "So am I, Morgan. I . . . I guess we're both a little testy after last night. And I'm much too sensitive about David. I'm still learning how to be a father to him."

She stepped toward him. "You . . . you're a wonderful father, Grant."

He laid his notepad aside and rose to refill his coffee. There was a heavy silence for long moments as they stood facing each other, coffee cups gripped tightly in anxious hands. Tightly he said, "Look, Morgan, this is a miserable way to begin the day. Let's try to forget what just happened." He turned on his heel and disappeared into the kitchen. "More coffee?" he called.

"Yes, please."

He ambled back and poured the steamy black liquid into her

47

waiting cup. She felt very bleak, knowing she had created the disturbance between them. An idea took form, and she heartened, thinking that perhaps she could salvage some semblance of their relationship.

Morgan sat on the couch opposite him, wrapping her hands around the warm cup which she set on her knees. "Grant, this has been a rough week. Since today is Sunday, let's take the day off and do something fun."

He raised dark brows. "What do you suggest?"

"Let's have a picnic! I know a great spot. David will love it and there's even a stream where we can fish! How about it, Grant?"

He smiled rigidly. "Okay, Morgan. It does sound like fun. And I know David would love it. Maybe we would enjoy it, too."

"Oh, we would . . . will! It's a beautiful place, Grant. I haven't been there in years, but we used to go there as kids. And I remember how much we loved it." She smiled happily, her eyes glowing with anticipation of a day spent with Grant.

They didn't bother with breakfast but packed a huge lunch for the picnic. David was content with a bowl of cereal, and babbled excitedly about the prospects of fishing. He helped Grant string the fishing rods for his first attempt at trout fishing. Expectations were high as they set out in the Suburban for the promised paradise in a hidden valley somewhere on the ranch.

It was one of those absolutely beautiful Colorado days in April with a perfect cerulean sky and brilliant sun to warm the early-morning chill. The tinge of frost that covered everything had melted, leaving a glistening accent on the world.

"What a gorgeous day! I'm glad we decided to do this! Aren't you, David?" Morgan smiled happily at David's bright face.

His large dark eyes were lustrous with excitement he could barely contain as he exclaimed, "I'm going to catch the biggest fish today! I can't wait! Can I cook him, Grant? Can I? How much longer till we get there?"

Grant's voice was teasing. "Now, wait just a doggone minute! You'll be competing with a champion trout fisherman today, David! You don't know what a great fisherman your dad is! But if you happen to catch any fish, of course you can cook them."

Morgan protested stoutly, "What makes you guys think

you're the only ones who can fish? I'll give you some stiff competition! Guaranteed!"

"Morgan?" David's voice was still timid around her. "Can you fish?"

"Sure." She grinned. "I'll show you. Turn here, Grant." She pointed to a narrow, almost obliterated road with two faint tire tracks. "It's been a long time since this road was traveled. Wonder if it's still passable."

"Sure, we can make it," Grant surmised as they bumped along on the old roadway.

"You know, David," Morgan recounted, "when I was a little girl, just about your size, my family used to come here for picnics. We'd spend all day fishing and playing games and hiking. It was such fun. . . ."

His small voice broke into her reminiscences. "Your father and mother brought you here?"

"Yes." She nodded, recalling those warm, carefree days.

"Just like today?" he asked innocently.

A knot lodged tightly in her throat as she nodded mutely, finally murmuring, "Yes, David. Just like today."

Suddenly the Suburban lunged sharply forward and ground to a halt. Quickly Grant started the motor and backed the vehicle out of the rut, then cut the engine again. "Well, folks," he announced, "this is as far as we go."

Morgan looked around. They were completely surrounded by shrubs. "That's okay. We're close to the stream. Seems to me this is as far as we ever drove. It's not very far, and we can just load up and walk. Can't we, David?"

"Sure. I'll carry the fishing rods! Let's go!" The beauty of excitement filled his small face, and the emotion of the previous moment was lost beyond his understanding.

"Here, son, you carry the rods. I'll get the food and cooler. Morgan, can you get the tackle box?" Grant distributed the various paraphernalia.

"Yay! I hear the water!" David grabbed the proffered fishing rods and took off with a hoot.

Morgan and Grant reached into the back of the Suburban at the same time for the remaining items. He grasped the portable cooler with one strong hand and glanced at Morgan.

49

"Need any help? Do we have it all?" He glanced down to see her clutching the tackle box in one hand, her other arm wrapped around a large, colorful quilt.

Their eyes met over the quilt and turbulent thoughts raced in both their minds. Grant broke the uneasy silence. "This was a good idea, Morgan. David loves it already."

She nodded, unable to smile as she looked into the depths of Grant's bold, blue-gray eyes. "I knew he would." She dropped her eyes, unwilling to meet his gaze any longer. Maybe this was a mistake for her.

"Is this hard for you, Morgan? Coming to this place so soon after your father's death?" His voice was serious and understanding.

A shrill voice echoed from beyond the tree line. "Grant! Come on!"

Morgan looked up quickly. "I'm fine, Grant. Let's go. David's going to catch the first fish before we even get there!"

And David did manage to catch the first fish! Then, amid great shouts of joy, he almost lost it. If it hadn't been for Grant's great fish-saving act, the fish would have been free again. But, true to a father's dedication, Grant lunged after the squirming fish, salvaging it for his young son. The fact that he had leaped into the ice-cold rushing stream was not important. The heroic act had prevented a catastrophe for David, and what did it matter that Grant's jeans were now thoroughly wet?

Both David and Morgan screeched with laughter and delight as they pulled their hero from the icy depths. He handed the slick fish to David with the admonition, "Last chance, son. Hold on to him this time." The meaning was clear to all. He would not dive into the chilling waters again.

"Oh, I will! Thanks, Grant! You saved my fish! Can I cook him? Can I?"

"Sure, son," Grant muttered through clenched teeth. He stood dripping water from drenched jeans that clung to his masculine shape.

Assured that the precious fish was safely in the creel, Morgan turned her attention to Grant. "Oh, my God, you're wet, Grant."

His eyes snapped at her. "Keen observance, Morgan!"

"If it'll make you feel any better, you were magnificent! You're now a hero! I'm sure David will never forget it. And neither will I." She couldn't control the peals of laughter that flooded her as she recalled his antics. "You should have seen it, Grant. Such great form! Why, the Denver Ballet Company would have been proud!"

He pushed past her, muttering for her ears only, "Doing a goddamn water ballet and freezing my ass off, and all you two can do is laugh!"

She couldn't resist quipping, "What do you expect us to do? Remove your pants and hang them on the line to dry?"

He turned around slowly to face her, an expression of bold vengeance on his face, and for a frantic minute she feared that is exactly what he would do. "Don't tempt me, my dear!" Then he wheeled around and stalked toward the Suburban.

"Where are you going, Grant?" Surely he wouldn't go back to the ranch so early and ruin their day.

"Oh, I wouldn't spoil your fun!" he called sarcastically. "Thank God I keep cutoffs in the jeep. Otherwise I could freeze my ass off, and you wouldn't care!"

"Oh, yes, we would!" Morgan answered, but he didn't acknowledge hearing her. So, she turned back to help David bait the hook for the next big battle. "Now, we're going to hold on to the next fish, aren't we, David?"

He nodded enthusiastically. "The next one . . . oh, boy!"

Grant returned shortly attired in a pair of very worn cutoff jeans. Morgan tried not to notice where the fringe graced the hard muscles of his legs as he climbed the rocks to just the right spot. He braced himself, and the corded muscles of his legs strained boldly as he cast his fishing line expertly into the dark holes. Undoubtedly he had fished for trout many times before, for he exhibited skillful knowledge as he quietly flicked his wrist and maneuvered the shiny artificial fly on the end of his line.

Meanwhile Morgan and David laughed and talked and scooted around on the lower rocks, clearly visible to any fish who might care to take notice of their loud, fun-filled activities. Yet they continued to pile up the fish and caught five between them in a period of two hours.

Morgan helped David untangle his line, and David returned

51

the favor by assisting when she caught her first fish. Morgan was so thrilled, she was shaking as she tried to unhook the squirming thing.

David bent over the prize with her, warning, "Don't drop it, Morgan. I don't think Grant will dive in the water again."

"I can guarantee it!" Grant's voice boomed behind them. "What's for lunch? I'm starved!"

Morgan dropped her fish pompously into the creel with David's catch and winked at the little boy. "Who cares about lunch? We have fish for supper! And David gets to cook them all!"

"Yay!" David clapped his hands in delight. "Morgan, I thought you came out here when you were a little girl," he chirped teasingly. He stood on a rock and towered above her blond braided hair.

She looked up curiously at him. "I did, David. I was just about your size."

He propped his hands on his hips and beamed down at her. "Well, I'm bigger than you! You're still a little girl! And lots more fun than Grant!"

"Little girl?" she sputtered, trying to tickle him before he jumped off the rock and dashed away, laughing at his own joke.

Grant howled with laughter and swatted her on the rear. "Come on, *little girl!* Let's eat! This man's starved!"

Chuckling, Morgan grabbed the quilt and followed her hungry fishermen, who were already trudging across the field.

"Over here!" yelled David, always ahead of them by at least twenty paces. "Let's eat here under this tree!"

As they approached the tree-shaded, grassy area, Grant agreed. "It looks just about perfect, David. Now, where's the food?"

Morgan spread the colorful quilt on the ground, and the three of them gathered around the food basket like rapacious predators scraping for sustenance.

"Stand back, you graceless vultures!" Morgan rebuffed. "I shall distribute this gourmet's delight in due turn. A sandwich for you and a pickle for you." She bowed first to David, then to Grant, both of whom obliged with large grins as the diminutive chef took charge.

"I thought you weren't inclined toward kitchen duties," Grant teased between bites of ham sandwich.

"Oh, I don't mind the gratification. It's the preparation I despise! And out here, this is fun! David, eat your sandwich before you start on the cookies."

Grant opened a diet soft drink and passed it to her. "It is fun, Morgan. This idea of yours was a good one."

"Well." She smiled. "I had to come up with something that would compare with the pizza night."

"This is funner," David said enthusiastically. "I like to fish!"

"I do, too. And I thought you would," Morgan agreed as she leaned back against the large tree trunk and sipped her drink. "Wow! I didn't realize how hungry I was! Is there another sandwich?"

"I knew you'd be starving by now. But I tried to restrain myself as long as I possibly could. Didn't want to ruin your fishing. That's my supper you're catching." Grant chuckled.

"And I get to cook them 'cause I caught the most!" chirped David, happily. "Can I go for a walk, Grant? Over there?" He pointed across the field.

Grant nodded. "If you stay within shouting distance. That means right around in the clearing so I can see you."

"Yes, sir," agreed David, grabbing a handful of cookies before he darted away.

Morgan shook her head in awe. "There he goes again. Where does he get the energy?"

"Well, he didn't stay up until after midnight last night drinking wine and talking!" Grant observed with a knowing smile. Emitting a thoracic groan, he eased himself to a reclining position and folded his hands under his head.

Morgan pulled her knees toward her chin and tried not to pay heed to the corded muscles bulging along his arms and chest. Those powerful arms had held her so soundly last night, easily eliciting her very feminine response to his masculine will. However she couldn't deny her own yearning for his touch. But that was last night when she was lulled by the wine and his virile appeal. After all she wasn't a zombie! Today, in clear light, she viewed things differently and she determined to let him know.

53

She looked away from him and studied the outline of trees against the azure sky. "Grant, about last night—"

His quick reply interrupted her words and train of thought. "Look, Morgan, I feel entirely responsible for that. I brought the wine, and initiated everything else. I can understand your position. If you don't want it to happen again, I can assure you it won't. I just find you attractive, and responded accordingly. If you don't like it, then . . ." He shrugged angular shoulders and shut his eyes. There was an air of indifference that infuriated Morgan. He had taken the words right out of her mouth, twisted their impact, and discounted their justification.

"It's not that I didn't like it . . . well, what I mean is—" She stopped abruptly. *Here I go again! Tongue-tied and stumbling over my words like a fool! Damn him, anyway!* "Grant, I just don't want that sort of thing to become a habit. I mean, that could be . . ."

"Dangerous?" He laughed. "Don't worry, Morgan. I'll back off. I can take a hint! Do you have someone else? Is there another man in your life? Just give me the word, and David and I can make ourselves very scarce."

"Oh, no." Her answer came too fast and she took a deep breath and tried to slow her words. "Not at the moment. Actually, I . . . while I was in Europe, most of my friends married."

He rolled over on his side, bending his arm to prop his head. "I mean it sincerely, Morgan. If you want a weekend in privacy, just say the word. We'll be gone in a second."

His seriousness about the rather pointed subject brought a warm blush to her cheeks, and she laughed lightly in an effort to ease her nervousness. "If the occasion arises, I'll be sure to let you know, Grant."

Grant smiled and nodded slightly in agreement with Morgan's blithe promise, those steely-gray eyes of his lingering over her knowingly. Then his gaze turned to encompass the majestic mountains that lined the horizon. "What a beautiful place to grow up. I would love for David to have this kind of freedom and fun. Look at him. He's really enjoying this, Morgan."

She grinned at the vision of the young, dark-haired boy chasing butterflies. "Hmmm . . . it is great for kids. I can remember romping through this field doing exactly what he's doing."

Grant took a deep breath. "Clean, fresh air . . . no smog. Peaceful and quiet . . . no cars honking or jets breaking the sound of silence. Did you come here often with your family?"

"When I was young, we came down here from Denver every holiday from school. Spent every summer here." She picked a long grass and chewed the sweet, juicy end. "When I was about ten—Do you want to hear this?" She stopped abruptly, unsure of his interest.

"Please go on, Morgan," he encouraged.

After a pause she continued. "Our mother died when I was about ten, leaving me as the only female in a very male-dominated family. My two brothers and father loved the winter sports available nearby and the country life the ranch provided. I was a part of those activities, too."

"Did you enjoy them?"

"Yes, but . . ." she answered slowly, "I suppose it wasn't enough for me. As I grew older, the peace and quiet was too dull for me. I wanted to travel."

"So, you took off for Europe," Grant added.

She shrugged. "Well, actually, in the last five or six years, none of us have used the ranch very much. My brothers were extremely busy with college and law school. I attended college for a few years, then had a chance to go to Europe with friends. I decided to quit school short of my degree, much to my father's chagrin."

"He wasn't in agreement with your decision to go to Europe?" Grant inclined his head toward her, detecting a growing terseness in Morgan's words.

"Of course, Daddy tried to convince me to finish college. Eventually, though, he agreed for me to use the rest of my education money for the trip. I guess my tour of Europe lasted longer than he expected. I was there three years. However I didn't realize just how much he was opposed to my . . . life-style . . . until he died."

After a moment Grant asked, "Did you come from Europe for your father's funeral, or were you here in the States?"

Somehow Morgan appreciated his sincerity. She hadn't talked much about her father's death and Grant seemed a willing listener. With a sigh she said, "I was in Amsterdam when I got the call. I hadn't seen him in three years. But he wasn't ill. The doctor said he probably had no symptoms before the sudden heart attack. He just died. It was quick." Her voice was flat. The pain of his death was still there, but had been dulled by her anger at his will.

Grant's voice was low and sober. "I'm sorry, Morgan. I know you and your father were close. Adam said you were your daddy's darling."

She nodded. "I thought we were close, too. But the will that Daddy left for us changed my mind about some things. Did Adam also tell you about that?" Morgan couldn't soften the hard tone that edged her voice.

He shook his head. "We didn't talk about the will."

She traced the colored shapes on the quilt aimlessly. "From the way the inheritance was distributed, you'd think he hated me."

"That bad?"

"For me, yes. Adam and Brett received the office buildings in Denver that are already money-producing real estate. I got this run-down ranch. All they have to do is maintain what's already functioning. I have to start from scratch."

"But just look at the challenge you have, Morgan! This place is beautiful . . . and promising."

Morgan's brown eyes glistened with hurt anger. Obviously Grant was just trying to bolster her. "To hell with challenge! Who wants to work so hard that you get calluses on your hands and blisters on your feet? Not me!"

Grant reached for her hand and pressed the palm to his lips, his tongue gently circling her sensitive flesh, sending tingles up her arm. His breath was soft and warm as he spoke into her hand. "That's what you hired me for, remember? I'm supposed to be the one to get calluses and blisters. And I still think you got a bargain." He kissed her palm, then turned it over to brush the rough knuckles with the softness of his lips.

Morgan tried to control her breathing as she answered, "You don't understand how Daddy has interfered in my life with his demands. He has just ruined it for me!" She tried to pull her hand away from Grant's tender, evocative caresses which were draining all rational conversation from her mind. "Please, don't do

56

that, Grant." Even though his lips and tongue had only grazed her hand, it was enough to stimulate alarming impulses inside her. His power was too magnetic for her to break away, and Morgan felt helplessly drawn to him.

Sitting up, he moved urgently closer, his arms enveloping her in a crushing embrace. "Morgan, Morgan, come to me . . ." His insistent words faded into a soft gasp just before his lips closed over hers. His tongue lightly teased her lower lip, then tickled the delicate outline of her upper lip, finally persuading her mouth to open for further intrusion.

At his touch Morgan immediately forgot her resolution of just moments before. Willingly she gave in to the soft pressure of his mouth, the tender probing of his tongue. The exquisite sensations that washed over her were too overpowering, too wonderful, to stop. Not just yet, anyway. She moved still closer to Grant; her fingertips playfully twirled the hairs at his nape. Grant, feeling her body melting into his, her soft feminine curves pressing against his tautening muscles, nuzzled his mouth along the sensitive line of her shoulder. Her hands began a slow dance of pleasure up and down his spine. This was like nothing else she had experienced. No one, not even André, had made her feel like this.

Grant slowly moved his mouth to repossess the softness of her lips, his probing tongue promising, urging, tempting. His warm hands slipped under her sweater, and reached around her ribs, his long fingers splayed against her sensitized flesh. As she clung to his shoulders, his hands shifted upward, gliding gently but skillfully over her soft breasts. His searching hands cupped each generous mound, and her sensitive tips swelled, drawing forth a surprised gasp from Morgan. Neither of them were aware of the small figure who galloped happily toward the shade tree.

"Hey, Grant! Look what I found!"

The small child's shrill voice stopped their passion cold and both Grant and Morgan jumped. Grant groaned softly and quickly pulled away from Morgan's warm body, folding his hands casually under his head. Morgan jerked back against the tree, tugging her sweater evenly around her hips.

"What, David?" Grant managed to mumble.

"See the grasshopper I caught?" David's shining face glowed blissfully while his grimy hand clutched a kicking green insect.

"That's great, son," Grant responded, showing amazing interest in the creature.

"Can we use it for fish bait? Are you ready to go fishing again?" Large, dark eyes looked down, questioning.

"Oh, uh, not yet, David. Why don't you see if you can catch a few more grasshoppers? Here, you can put them in this empty sandwich bag."

David eagerly complied with his father's request and brought a smile to Grant's face as he ran off again. There was an uneasy silence and a sudden gust rustled the leaves of the shade tree.

Grant's steel-gray eyes met hers. "Morgan, I—"

Morgan shifted her position and gazed at him honestly. "You don't have to explain, Grant. It . . . it was as much my fault as yours. But it just can't keep happening. I have a ranch to run and . . . you have your work. At this rate the place will never make it."

"Perhaps your father left you the ranch because he had confidence that you could build it into something beautiful as well as useful."

"With the stipulations surrounding the damn thing, I have to make it work . . . or lose it. Oh, yeah, he forced me to do what he wanted." Resentment steeled her voice.

"What do you mean by that? What stipulations?" Grant puzzled.

"Well, part of the provisions are that I have to make the ranch profitable within a year, or share the ownership with my brothers. If I just let it sit, believe me, I'll lose it. They'll take over."

"Profitable in a year? That's damn near impossible for any business, especially a tourist-oriented one. My God, Morgan— how could he do that to you?" Grant's voice rose as he sat up, looking at her in amazement. "So that's why you're so determined to pull this thing together in a hurry."

Morgan's eyes flashed deep bronze in her angry response. "You're damned right I am! I'm determined that this is one thing they won't run in my life! They've tried, already. Adam was willing to help, which was fine. But when he broke his leg, Brett called to tell me to return home until they could help me. See, they still want to keep me under their thumb! Just like my father did! That's what Daddy intended when he left the will so confined in legalities."

"Do you think he was pushing you to independence?"

She looked at Grant curiously. How much did he actually know about her? She admitted, "He wanted me to settle down to one thing. And to stay in this country." Did she dare say "settle down to one person"? "With this will, he has forced me to change my life and do what he wanted me to do. And I resent that. My brothers weren't forced to change anything. Their lives are the same . . . or better. They now have additional income and property."

"Don't forget," Grant advised, "they also have additional responsibilities. Keeping businesses going isn't easy, Morgan."

She sighed. "Oh, I know that. But apparently Daddy didn't think I could handle a business, so he gave me this stupid ranch. And even that is dampened by restrictions. Thank God there's also a trust fund set up for me and I can borrow from it without cosignatures from my dear brothers!"

Suddenly Grant's features were alive with enthusiasm. "Morgan, in all modesty, we have made an excellent start on the ranch. And I love the challenge of what can be done with it. I'd like to help you make a profitable business of it. Now, I don't know if it'll be earning its own way this summer. That seems a little too soon. But we can give it a try! How about it? I told you I'd stay the summer. And I will. I believe we can make it if we work together!"

Morgan looked at him doubtfully. Why was he so eager to help her? Was it the challenge—or her? "Of course, Grant, I would love to show Adam and Brett that I can be successful without their influence. But I don't know . . ."

Confidence was evident as Grant encouraged her. "Together we can do it, Morgan! I'm sure of it!"

She smiled at his little-boy zeal. "Grant, you don't know anything about ranching and neither do I."

He shrugged. "We'll learn together. Now let's go find my son before he catches all the grasshoppers here!" He caught her hand and they ran across the green, grassy field . . . together.

* * *

59

Although the hour was late, Morgan paced the living room. Her thoughts were jumbled, confused, wrangling inside her until she could scream. She reflected on the day spent with Grant and David. It had been glorious, a time to remember with joy. And then there was the arrangement she and Grant had discussed. Actually she could find no fault with someone wanting to help her. It gave her some assurance and peace of mind regarding the ranch. But another thought had been tearing at her mind since their agreement. If he was going to stay the summer, then why not—? No! How could she? She hardly knew him! And yet she would have to do something . . . sometime. That was another proviso of the will. One that she hadn't told Grant. She could offer him the stability that he needed for David as well as the fifty-thousand-dollar wedding gift. It would be worth the money to her, for she had no great need of it. But Grant did. Would he do it?

Beleaguered by her own wildly racing thoughts, she roamed through the large ranch house. If she could convince him that he would benefit, too, then maybe he would help her. She glanced out the back window nervously. A small yellow glow outlined the bunkhouse door. He was still awake! Well, why not try?

With sweating palms Morgan gripped the doorknob and bolted across the backyard to the bunkhouse. She would simply try before she lost the nerve. Gnawing questions continued to bedevil her even as she approached the smaller building. What if . . . he refused? What if . . . he left her now? What if he wouldn't even stay the duration of the summer to work? What if . . . this ruined everything?

What if . . . oh, God . . . he said *yes*?

Morgan paused for a moment to gather her strength and listened to the clicking of his typewriter in the quiet night. He was working . . . poor guy. After all the toil of this exhausting week he still tried to write! Didn't that prove his need for the deal she was about to propose?

She knocked lightly on the door and waited, dread engulfing her like a chilling fog. The typing stopped and Morgan held her breath. She could hear him walking across the floor, but wasn't quite prepared for his rugged, masculine figure outlined in the open doorway. His shirt hung loosely, unbuttoned and barely hiding the crisply curling mat that spread across his chest.

"Morgan? What's wrong?"

"Grant, I—" When she finally found her voice, it came out embarrassingly shaky.

"Morgan, are you all right?" Grant's hand reached out to her, and, incredibly, she moved away from him. He placed his outstretched hand on the door facing, obviously perplexed by her strange behavior.

She had to say something to him! She was here before him! Oh, God, what would this do to her life? With a rush of breath and courage she expelled, "Grant, will you marry me?"

CHAPTER FOUR

The shocked expression on Grant's face disclosed all Morgan needed to know at the moment. Grant was appalled, angered, probably even repulsed by her question. He would depart as soon as he could gather his son and their meager belongings. Morgan was sure of it. She had destroyed what little working relationship they had. It would never be the same even if he stayed. But he wouldn't do that. Couldn't. Now he would leave her alone on the ranch—in fear of having his already difficult life completely ruined by this crazy female who asked for his hand in marriage after knowing him only one week.

Unsteadily Morgan turned away from him, bitter tears stinging her eyes. She hated this degradation—all because of her father and his unreasonable demands. Damn him!

As she started away, she heard Grant's laughter. He was actually laughing at her . . . amused at her ignoble invitation to marriage. Damn him, too! Oh, how she hated him! His low laughter rang in her head until she wanted to scream. And run. So that is exactly what she did—or tried to do.

Forceful, masculine hands restrained her efforts, gripping her, wrapping her into his steel-hard arms . . . warm, secure arms that had held her before. Only now they seemed to be binding her, coercing her into the shame of confronting him. His hand cupped her chin, lifting the angry-sad face so that he could see the tears that trailed her cheeks.

His voice was harsh. "Morgan, what did you say?"

She clinched her teeth, determined not to cry anymore—and not to humiliate herself before this man again. Once was enough —more than enough for Morgan Cassity.

"Get your hands off me!"

His breath was frosty in the cold night air as he rasped, "Don't run away from me, then! Talk to me, Morgan! It's not often that I'm asked to marry. And I want to know why. It's not for love!"

She almost spat her words. "No! It's not for love! It's for . . . for business!"

"What?"

Morgan's sable eyes flashed at him wildly. Oh, why had she ever done such a thing? "I . . . it's . . . oh, why don't you just go on and leave me alone? It's what you want to do! Just pack up and get out of here! Then you can laugh all you want to! Oh, yes, Grant LeMaster, you can laugh about the hysterical female who asked you to marry her one miserable night! And let go of me! You're hurting my arms!"

He eased up slightly on her arms, but didn't let go completely. "Then let's go into the house and talk about this. I'm intrigued by your question. And curious about your reason."

"And don't forget amused by the idea!" she hissed.

"No more laughter, I promise."

"I have nothing to say to you." She regretted even mentioning it, hoping he would let the subject drop . . . knowing he would not.

"I'm interested in the proposal," he persisted.

Morgan's eyes narrowed, as she doubted his sincerity. "It would make great writing material, wouldn't it?"

With a resigned shrug Grant's arms slumped to his sides. "I wouldn't do that to you, Morgan. Surely you know that."

Now that she was free from his fierce grasp, Morgan turned away from him. How could she trust him? She didn't even know him. And she had been fool enough to ask this strange man to be her husband!

Grant's ragged voice broke the stillness of the night. "Morgan, what if I said yes? Yes, I'll marry you."

She stopped midstep and took in a shaky breath. Had she really heard right?

63

"Morgan, the answer is yes." The steel edge of his voice cut into her, and she knew she had to answer him. But what could she say? How could she explain? Did she really want this?

Morgan's voice was unsteady as she asked, "Are . . . are you sure?"

"Frankly, no! How the hell can I be sure when I hardly know you? But I do know one thing. You're in trouble or you would never have posed such a wild proposition. Maybe I can help you a little, Morgan. Are you pregnant?"

"No!" She wheeled around to face Grant and encountered his darkly concerned face and long arms folded across his chest. He was just like all the others. Maybe Adam had done too much talking to his friend. Maybe he told Grant she had spent the last few years in Europe . . . with different men! Oh, how could he? "No, I'm not pregnant! And I'm not in trouble!"

"Then why do you want me to marry you?"

"I don't! I mean . . . er . . . I can't help it!"

"Can't help it? You have a compulsion for marriage?" Amusement played at his lips, infuriating her further.

"No, I certainly do not! And I would never have asked you if I hadn't been out of my mind . . . temporarily, that is! Now I'm sane again, so just forget it!"

"Ah, you're too late to rescind the proposal. You've asked, and I've accepted! Now let's go inside before we freeze, and discuss the upcoming nuptials!" He steered her firmly but gently toward the back door of the ranch house, and before she knew it, they were sipping hot chocolate and she was pouring out the entire miserable story of the stipulations in her father's will.

"So it would be a union for business purposes only. There would be none of the . . . uh . . . usual privileges of a marriage," Morgan explained tactfully.

Grant looked at her sharply. "Do you mean sexual privileges?"

Her eyes met his defiantly. "Exactly."

He shrugged. "My concern was regarding the sharing of property and . . . custody."

His attitude afforded considerable relief. At least he wouldn't bother her about sex. "David?" She hadn't even thought of the boy. "Oh, I would never interfere with your relationship with your son, Grant."

"I'd want it in writing."

She shrugged. "Fifty thousand is mine—ours—upon marriage. I will give it all to you if you'll stay long enough to get the ranch working smoothly, say, the end of the summer. At that time you can have the money. No strings attached. But I want to retain the ranch in my name. And I'd want it in writing."

He pursed his lips thoughtfully. "Sounds reasonable. You keep the ranch, I keep the kid. By the end of the summer we should be even. Is it a deal?"

Morgan nodded in full agreement. "It's a deal!" She smiled wanly and extended her hand. Their hands clasped to seal the strangest arrangement either had ever dreamed of . . . in all their traveling or writing. The run-down little Colorado ranch would be the location of the most unique and unusual summer either had ever experienced.

The next day they went into town for the necessary blood tests that would precede the bizarre arrangement-marriage. They talked to a lawyer who would draw up the marriage agreement they both would sign, detailing the items they desired. There were some basic issues here, and love was definitely not one of them.

Morgan and Grant rode back to the ranch in strained silence, each seemingly lost in sober contemplation. Finally Grant suggested, "Morgan, I think it's about time we considered hiring some additional help. We'll certainly need it when time grows closer to opening the ranch, and it would be nice if we had someone by then that we knew and could trust. I could use some help now with the corrals and barns, and I'm sure you could use help in the house."

Morgan looked at Grant sharply. "Let's get something straight right now. The house is *not* my domain! I will not be in charge of the kitchen! Nor of the house!"

"Nor the bedroom?" He chuckled.

"Right!" she reaffirmed adamantly.

"Well, then, it's time we hired someone to be in charge of the kitchen! And the house as well!" A muscle twitched menacingly in his tight jaw, and Morgan grinned at the reactions apparent in his very masculine profile.

She just couldn't resist taunting him. "And what about the bedroom? Do you have someone in mind?" A mocking sweetness dripped from her voice as she folded her arms and glared at him, waiting for an answer. She would be damned if she would allow his liaisons on her ranch, and they may as well get that straightened out right now.

"I'll keep my bedroom activities as discreet as you do," he answered brusquely. "As for the rest of the house and grounds, yes, I do have someone in mind. I know an older couple who live in Durango and are having a tough time making a living these days. He's an old ranch hand and cowboy with a multitude of skills, but people are reluctant to hire him anymore because of his age. I think a ranch the size of yours would be just about perfect for him. And I'm sure his wife would be willing to take over the kitchen duties, including early-morning breakfast."

Morgan listened intently, ignoring the jabs at his discreet bedroom activities and her awful early-morning breakfast attempts. The fact was they *had* reached a point when they both needed more help around the ranch. And they definitely would be hiring someone in a month or so. Why not now? Plus, it would be nice to have someone else, besides David, on the premises to ensure they weren't completely alone after the marriage. Grant would be forced to go elsewhere for his "discreet bedroom activities." He wouldn't dare flaunt his promiscuity in front of them.

Morgan nodded in agreement. "I certainly agree that we need help. And this couple you know sounds suitable. I'd like to meet them before a final decision is made, though."

"Certainly. I'll arrange it for our next trip into town," Grant allowed.

"Good. Then maybe he could help you get the wild horses down at Ignacio," Morgan replied.

"Wild horses?" The vehicle lurched a little.

Morgan smiled sheepishly. "Actually, it was Adam's idea to buy unbroken horses and break them ourselves for saddle or pack. They're cheaper. So I bought a couple of horses from a rancher near Ignacio. Grant, they're not wild . . . just a little green. They don't take to riders well yet."

"My God, Morgan! Do you know how goddamn much trouble unbroken horses can be?"

She shrugged and answered honestly, "Never thought much about it."

His tone showed his agitation. "Well, hell, woman! Who's going to break them?" The minute he said it, *he knew!*

She paused before saying, "Who's in charge of the corrals?"

"I'll be damned! It's been years since I've saddle-broken a horse! Do you want me to kill myself?" He was still quite impassioned.

Morgan raised her eyebrows and quipped, "Not before the wedding. I figured if I took care of renovation and purchasing, you could handle training . . . and early breakfasts for the Rocking M Ranch!"

"Rocking M Ranch? Seems to me you should name it Lazy M Ranch—that would be closer to the truth!" Grant scoffed.

"Now, now, darling. Don't be bitter! Can you believe we're having our first lover's quarrel? And we aren't even married yet!" Morgan figured she had pushed Grant about as far as she could in this first bout. After all, she knew she needed him. His business sense would prove valuable, as would his strong back. But he had a stake in this project, too. It was to his benefit to make the endeavor profitable by summer's end. Then he could leave with the fifty thousand, free and clear. Not a bad salary for a summer's work. And Morgan could go about her life, free of the entanglement of a husband. It couldn't come too soon for her. But first Morgan had a wedding to attend. Her own!

Morgan stared at the distant, white-tipped mountain peaks. They were so steady and peaceful and constant . . . always there, always dependable. Their steadfast significance gave her the strength she needed to endure this, her wedding day.

Grant would return soon. He had surprised her by saying that he and David should be dressed appropriately for the wedding. The two of them headed for town early, with a promise to return soon for her. She didn't know why he wanted to bother with a suit for this facade of a wedding, but it forced her to thinking of wearing something besides her jeans and velour sweater. Maybe he thought of himself as a "landed gentry" now and felt he should dress as befitting someone of his status. Ha! She supposed she would raise his status considerably with this marriage. Just for the hell of it, she should wear her scrubbiest clothes. She smiled involuntarily at the thought. It would serve him right!

The noise of a vehicle in the driveway attracted her attention, and Morgan turned away from the glorious mountains. Sure enough, there were Grant and David climbing out of the burgundy Suburban. They were both dressed to the teeth. Even little David sported a pair of new leather cowboy boots, beige slacks, and a dark brown sport jacket with western cut to the coat. It fit his little shoulders perfectly, and he looked so handsome. When he turned around, she could see that his small, dark face was aglow with a broad smile.

Oh, God, what was all this going to do to David? She hadn't even considered him until this moment. What was he thinking? Did he want her as his new mother? *Mother!* She had not even talked to him about it and wondered what Grant had told him. It had all happened so fast, they had not really discussed the boy. All she knew was that she wasn't to interfere with the custody of David when the divorce came about. But that didn't mean she couldn't be friends with him. Maybe not a mother—she shuddered at the thought. But they could be friends.

The joyous expression on David's face was too much for Morgan. She just couldn't ruin his day by dressing in her oldest clothes. She dropped her robe and opened the closet door, searching for something appropriate . . . something *comme il faut*. Her eyes fell on an exquisite designer dress that she had purchased in Paris last year. She had only worn it a few times—Once to a friend's wedding and again in Greece with André. *André.* She had bought it with André in mind . . . knowing he would love it. Her bronze eyes flickered at the memories, acknowledging bitterly that it now seemed justifiable to wear the ivory-colored garment to her wedding. Morgan quickly slipped her arms into the long sleeves which were cuffed tightly with tiny, pearl buttons at the wrists. The bodice clung softly to her curves, caressing the swell of her bosom. It was impossible to avoid the creamy stretch of cleavage visible in the deeply plunging V neckline. A small, tie-belt hugged the slim waistline she had hidden all week under jeans and a bulky shirt. Morgan surveyed her reflection in the full-length mirror, wondering briefly if the dress was too seductive for her wedding. She turned, and the skirt swirled gently around her knees, brandishing beautiful, cutwork embroidery. Splendid! It's not too alluring, she decided. Just impressive. Maybe Grant would find his new bride attractive in this. She smiled wryly to herself. *Why do I care what Grant thinks of me? This is just a business deal for both of us.*

She ran a brush through her flaxen hair, letting it hang loosely over her shoulders. Maybe David wouldn't be too ashamed to have her for a new mother, even if she was only temporary. She sighed heavily. *Well, let's get on with it!* Morgan opened the front door, where David and Grant stood waiting. There was a clumsy silence as the trio stood under one another's visual scrutiny.

David was the first to speak. "Wow, Morgan! You look beautiful! Why don't you wear that dress here at the ranch?" His innocent honesty embarrassed her.

Morgan blushed prettily, avoiding the gleam of approval and unhidden desire in Grant's eyes. Purposely she spoke to David. "Thank you, David. You look so handsome today, I felt I should wear something nice to accompany you."

"Well, it's sure nice, isn't it, Grant?" David's dark eyes glistened brilliantly at his father as he reached for Grant's hand.

"Oh, it's . . . very . . . nice," agreed Grant, with a wicked grin for Morgan and a wink for little David.

Morgan was amazed at David's reactions to her appearance. Was the kid wise beyond his years? Or was he wise because of living with a bachelor father? Well, what should she expect? The man who was to be her husband stood there agog, his slate-gray eyes fairly bugging out of his head. Maybe the dress had done more than it was meant to. She certainly didn't want him to think . . . But that had been spelled out with clarity. Morgan lifted her chin proudly to meet his steady gaze.

Grant's knowing eyes roamed down the V neck of her dress, then back to her flushed cheeks. "Yes, Morgan. I'm very fortunate to be standing by your side today. You are gorgeous, even if you are a little girl." He reached to take her hand, but she brushed by him coolly.

"Spare me the hearts and flowers, Grant. It will do you no

good. Besides, we both know what this is all about," she muttered close to him.

Undaunted, he managed to open the Suburban door before she could reach it. "Speaking of flowers, I thought you should have a bouquet for your wedding." He produced a small assemblage of tiny forget-me-nots surrounding a white orchid and thrust it into her hands.

Instinctively her fingers lightly caressed the smooth petals of the orchid. It was a beautiful gesture and Morgan was touched. "Thank you, Grant," she murmured, keeping her head lowered as she climbed into the front seat. It wouldn't do for him to see the sudden swelling of tears that filled her eyes. Did he really care? He seemed to be trying to make this a special day. Sighing, she wondered if anyone really cared that she was being forced into a marriage today. Her family didn't even know. It had been decided that they would be notified later.

The trip into town was extremely quiet and strained. Morgan tried to ignore the fact that Grant looked very dashing in his beige, camel-hair blazer with stitched detailing and double-point back yoke. His champagne-colored silk shirt was complemented by a western bolo tie with silver concho slide inset with a huge turquoise stone. The thing must have cost him a fortune, unless it was a gift from his former wife's family.

Under normal conditions Morgan wouldn't even attempt to hide her admiration for the handsome man beside her. But these weren't normal conditions. She felt doomed to endure a marriage she never wanted . . . with a man she hardly knew. And she was definitely the reluctant bride.

The strange marriage contract was signed first, the stipulations in agreement with both parties. He wouldn't interfere with her property. She wouldn't contest his child custody. They stood somewhat nervously before the justice of the peace, who was, surprisingly enough, a woman. She read the age-old vows methodically from a dog-eared little book, smiling presumptuously at the tall, steely man and serious young woman before her. Their stony expressions didn't change throughout the short ceremony.

When she reached the part about the ring, Morgan gazed uncertainly at Grant. It hadn't even occurred to her that a ring

70

would be necessary. However Grant smoothly reached into his pocket and produced a small round thing which he proceeded to slip onto her finger, repeating something about "with this ring I thee wed."

Morgan looked down and gasped silently. Wrapped around her finger was an absolutely beautiful crafting in silver with inlays of deep, dark turquoise. Her startled bronze eyes raised to meet Grant's just as the justice of the peace entoned, "All right, you may kiss your bride." *It was done!*

Morgan watched as his taut face approached hers, bearing down, closer and closer until she felt his warm lips on hers, tenderly claiming his wife before witnesses. The long moments were finally interrupted by loud applause and cheering from their smallest spectator. "Yay! It's over! Now can we get some ice cream like you promised, Morgan?"

Grant released her then, and Morgan turned from her husband to look at David with a grateful smile. "Sure, David. I think I'll celebrate with Doom's Day Licorice!"

As they left the building, Morgan slowed, purposely allowing David to run on ahead. She touched Grant's arm with her left hand, where the ring gleamed boldly, almost ostentatiously.

"Grant . . ." she began hesitantly. "You really shouldn't have gone to all this expense. The ring is . . . just magnificent." Her sable eyes were large and round and serious.

His unwavering gaze settled on her. *Those eyes . . . those beautiful, blue-gray eyes.* "I couldn't find a diamond I liked on such short notice."

She shrugged. "Diamonds are forever, like the ad says. And we both know this marriage is just temporary. Is it turquoise? I don't think I've ever seen turquoise so green." She held the ring out admiringly.

He nodded tersely. "That ring has a legacy, Morgan. The reason the stone is so rich and green instead of the usual turquoise blue is that it came from a special mine in Utah. Thunder Mountain turquoise is very valuable today because that mine has been closed for about twenty years. So it's rare."

Morgan pursed her lips as she examined the ring anew. "How interesting. And the legacy?"

Grant took her hand and cradled it tenderly in his own, looking deeply into her eyes. "It is said that the one who wears this ring will be forever loved." He lifted her fingers to his lips and kissed them repeatedly.

As his lips played sensuously with her fingertips, she asked nervously, "Do you believe that myth?"

He shrugged with a slight smile. "We could make it happen."

She shook her head vigorously, knowing what he was insinuating. Then a terrible thought struck her, and with a shaky voice Morgan asked, "It didn't belong to David's mother, did it?"

His fingers tightened on hers. "Hell no! I bought it for a very beautiful woman, my wife. The ring is yours, Morgan. Make of it what you will!" Grant dropped her hand and turned away, leaving her feeling like a first-class heel.

She grasped for his arm. "I . . . Grant, I'm sorry. I didn't mean to diminish its intent. I'll wear the ring . . . proudly." She managed a faint smile.

A childish voice interrupted calling loudly, "Grant, Morgan, are you ever coming?"

"Sure, son, we'll be right there," Grant replied.

"Grant"—Morgan gripped his arm as she watched the small boy wistfully—"I hope David doesn't get hurt by all this."

Grant's voice was matter-of-fact. "We'll all be affected by this marriage of ours, Morgan. There's no way we can avoid it. The acts of adults always affect the children, in one way or another. But I'll do everything I can to protect David as much as possible. I only hope you'll do the same." Grant started walking and Morgan followed.

Yes, they all would be affected by this marriage . . . and maybe even hurt. Nothing that manipulated people's lives ever left them completely unscathed. She knew it, and now felt guilty because she had dragged little David into her business marriage. Very guilty.

However if Grant cared so much for his son, why had he been willing to enter into the deal? The answer was clear. There was a large amount of money in this agreement for him. Grant had money to gain and nothing to lose . . . only time.

The fingers on her right hand involuntarily caressed the silver wedding ring. Morgan sighed and followed her new husband. Summer wouldn't end soon enough for her.

After the ice cream it was business as usual as they stopped by to meet and hire the older couple Grant had recommended. Boyd Simpson was a wiry, lean man in his late fifties. He had a ready smile and walked with a limp. Grant arranged to meet him the next morning to travel to Ignacio for the unbroken horses.

Willa Simpson, Boyd's wife, was a simple, happy woman who tousled David's hair affectionately and agreed to manage the ranch house, and especially the kitchen. Morgan could tell they would have a great alliance. She liked the Simpsons at first meeting and admitted ruefully that Grant was right about them. They would be good additions to the Rocking M.

Morgan and Grant spent the afternoon of their wedding putting the finishing touches on the repaired corral and barn in preparation for the first influx of animals the following day. By nightfall David was eager for his bath and bed. As usual Grant took care of the child, tucking him in bed in the bunkhouse. Morgan thought she had seen the last of her husband as she slumped exhaustedly in front of the unlit fireplace. She sat alone, begrudgingly recalling that this was her wedding day . . . and night. She was feeling very sad and melancholy when she heard a sharp knock at the back door, followed by the definite sounds of someone entering.

"Morgan?" Grant's voice questioned.

It was only her husband. *Husband!* How strange the word sounded.

Without even glancing up she acknowledged him. "Yes? What do you want?"

"Just thought we'd celebrate. After all, it is our wedding night."

She looked up sharply then and caught sight of the bottle of champagne he brandished. "Celebrate what? My compliance?"

His answer was just as sharp as hers. "*Your* compliance? What about mine?" He set the bottle on the kitchen counter and began to work diligently on the cork.

Morgan's tart voice followed him there. "You? You haven't been compromised! You have nothing to lose! And only money to gain! Not a bad deal, Grant LeMaster!"

The cork popped loudly, punctuating her remarks.

Quietly he crossed the room and bowed graciously as he handed her a glass of the bubbly liquid. "For you, Mrs. LeMaster." His tone was smoothly vicious. "And you have nothing to lose but the ranch! Shall I leave now? You can pick up the wild horses with Boyd tomorrow. And you can break them yourself. And you can—"

"All right, Grant! I do need you. And I realize you're here at my request. Actually I'm very grateful that you'd be willing to marry me . . . someone in my condition!" Her eyes softened.

His eyes traveled over her, and his tone was debasing. "Are you trying to tell me that you are pregnant, after all?"

She laughed mockingly at his angry tone, enjoying the tingling on the tip of her nose as she took a drink of the champagne. "I told you I'm not pregnant. I just meant the conditions of my father's will. There aren't many who would be willing to take a wife under those conditions. Of course, I've tried to make it profitable to you. You're a little edgy tonight, husband dear."

"Just matching your mood, my sweet little wife."

Morgan stared defiantly into his belligerent eyes, then turned away to the empty, black fireplace. In a moment she spoke. Gone was the bite in her tone and, in its place, a touch of melancholy. "Look, Grant, I'm afraid I'm a little bitter tonight. This is not the way I had imagined my marriage would be, and I'll admit, I'm not in a very good mood. I had hoped for love somewhere along the way. I . . . I don't want you to leave the ranch, Grant. You know I need you this summer. I guess I'm just a little uptight tonight."

"Believe it or not, I can understand what you're saying, Morgan." He motioned to refill her glass. "Drink up, darling. It'll help you relax. You sound as though you need it."

Morgan's sorrel eyes narrowed distrustingly. "So I'll be more agreeable to grant you sexual favors on your wedding night?"

His taunting grin infuriated her. "I don't expect any favors. You made that perfectly clear at the beginning, Morgan."

She sat up straight, her blond hair swinging furiously across one shoulder. "And I meant it, too! Oh, you've been very nice all day. But all the champagne and nice flowers and beautiful rings in the world won't make me change my mind!"

Grant leaned his head back and gulped long and loud, emptying the glass before turning his devil-like eyes on her. "Oh, I don't expect the virtues of life to change your hostile mind, Morgan! It'll be pure, unadulterated *lust* that does the trick! Enjoy your celebration alone, Mrs. LeMaster." He turned on his heel and strode out, leaving Morgan to spend her wedding night in silent isolation.

CHAPTER FIVE

"They're back, Morgan! The truck is here! Come on! Let's see the horses they brought! Oh, boy!" David's small, bright face flashed through the darkening shadows of evening as he darted off to greet Grant and the new ranch foreman, Boyd Simpson.

Her muscles aching, Morgan laid aside the pitchfork and surveyed the area where she had spread fresh, sweet-smelling straw for the new animals. She smiled to herself, proud of a job well done. Yes, they had done a lot in the last week toward turning the run-down ranch into a workable one. Most of the work had centered on getting the barn and corral ready for these horses. She and David had helped Grant with the repairs, hammering on stalls, doors, and feeders. Living, or rather, working together had been somewhat strained for a day or two after the wedding. But there was so much work to be done, they had adopted a brother-sister relationship. It was an easy posture to assume, since theirs was certainly not a typical husband-wife alliance.

Today, while Grant hauled the new horses from Ignacio, she had been in charge of cleaning the stalls, spreading clean hay on the floor, and stocking the oats in the feed bin. She had completed the tasks and was satisfied that everything was ready for the new animals. Grant would be pleased. *Why does it matter what he thinks?* she wondered stubbornly. *It shouldn't. But it does.*

Morgan looked down at her red, raw hands. The palms burned

unpleasantly. She turned them over and examined the broken blisters. With a pang of regret she remembered the time Grant had kissed those palms so tenderly and promised he would be the one getting blisters and calluses. That was before their marriage, though. Things were different now. He didn't care about her blisters.

Confident that the old barn was fully prepared for their first animals, Morgan started toward the happy sounds of David and the two men. She knew that danger as well as immediate responsibilities came with the acquisition of the unbroken horses. Grant had reminded her about the real necessity for insurance for the ranch. It was a detail that she had never been concerned with. But now, with animals on the property and employees as well, their liability was great. What would she have done without Grant here to make sure about these things?

However these new responsibilities were indications that the dude ranch was becoming a reality, not just an idea. And she had to admit, if only to herself, that Grant had been a major contributor to that reality. Bitter as their exchanges had been, Morgan had confidence that Grant would stay and work through the summer. After all, he had committed himself. And so had she. The silver and turquoise wedding ring gracing her third finger was proof of that.

Morgan rounded the corner of the barn, and a small fist of desire knotted in her stomach as she caught sight of Grant. Even in the growing shadows of evening, she could see those mesmeric gray eyes and the squareness of his jawline as he worked to open the back of the huge truck they had rented for hauling the horses. He was lean and ruggedly appealing, looking every inch a cowboy tonight. It was hard to believe his claim to be a writer. Morgan bit her lip in frustration at her own sudden desires. Oh, lord, he was handsome! If only she weren't so indebted to him . . . if only she hadn't been forced into marrying him . . . perhaps he would appeal to her. Well, hell! Who was she trying to fool, anyway! He *did* appeal to her! She was inexorably drawn to this arrogant, virile man she had married, even though she fought against this primitive urge. She just couldn't help it! If only they could get along!

Grant turned toward her and their eyes met for a moment in

the dusky light. It was no more than a brief hesitation, but the impact left Morgan unnerved and puzzled, wondering what he was thinking about this strange, stubborn bride he had taken. If she knew, she would possibly be astounded. Possibly . . .

Without betraying his thoughts Grant uttered a low, muffled greeting, but continued with his chore, giving her no more attention than a fence post.

However the older man caught the glance and mistook it for something else. He grabbed the chains on the truck and muttered roughly, "Go on, son. Tell her hello like you mean it. I'll get this." By his statement Boyd had made the situation obvious, leaving Grant no alternative but to comply.

So he stepped awkwardly to Morgan, his disdainful eyes cutting into her. Oh, how he must hate her! As he moved close for the kiss she knew was coming, she closed her eyes and flinched inwardly at his touch. A rough hand reached for her shoulder and warm lips grazed her face, ever so close to her lips, yet not quite on them. He had purposely avoided their contact, but she was the only one who knew. He obligingly endured the kiss, just as she did. Having others around was going to be more difficult than she had figured. Could she endure this marriage farce? And it was just beginning!

"Come and see the horses you bought. They're fine-looking animals," he estimated. Grant's attention to her was minimal, as he was far more interested in getting the snorting, restless animals out of the van.

Moving the agitated horses proved to be a hectic job, with both men straining for control, Morgan opening gates, and David wide-eyed with excitement. He seemed to be everywhere at once —in front, behind, in each doorway—always in the wrong place at the wrong time. The horses were excited and nervous, and all three adults pulled David out of the way of sharp hooves at least once. Grant's calm instructions to the child went unheeded until finally in exasperation the father exploded, "All right, David! No more moving around! Stay right where you are and don't move. You're in the way and going to get hurt!"

It must have been the first time Grant had raised his voice to David, for the boy looked as though he had been struck. Recoiling with real trepidation coupled with embarrassment, David ran out of the barn.

__"David! David!" called Grant, as he latched the final stall.

Morgan followed the upset child far enough to see him enter his room in the bunkhouse. But Grant's harsh voice halted her continued progress.

"I'll handle him, Morgan."

She wheeled around and snapped, "Now look what you've done! You were too harsh with him!"

His eyes narrowed. "He purposely disobeyed me!"

"Well, did you have to yell at him like that? He was excited. He's just a little kid, Grant!"

"I expect him to obey me, especially when it regards his safety! I didn't want him trampled by wild horses!" Grant propped his fists on his hips and glared at her.

Morgan matched his aggressive stance. "Neither did I! But that's no way to talk to him."

"I'll deal with my son as I see fit. And I don't expect you to interfere! *Comprende?*" Grant's tone was hard.

"Oh, I understand perfectly well. You are such a pig-headed mule, nobody can tell you a thing! Even when you're wrong!"

"If you'll shut up and move out of my way, I can go and talk with David!"

"What are you going to do—apologize?" Morgan mocked. "That certainly doesn't sound like the stubborn jackass I know!"

"That's part of the problem, Morgan. You don't know me at all!" he asserted through clenched teeth. Brushing past her, he headed resolutely for the bunkhouse.

"But I married you anyway," Morgan murmured miserably, half to herself. An overpoweringly ominous feeling that she had made a very big mistake settled over her like a huge net. And she was trapped in the middle of that net with no way to escape.

Morgan slammed the door to her room. She was so agitated after her confrontation with Grant that her eyes smarted with angry tears and her stomach churned nervously. Never had she felt so frustrated and helpless in her entire, pampered life. Morgan paced the floor, feeling like a trapped animal. She glanced up at her reflection in the mirror. *And a wild animal, that,* she mused wearily. Her hair had been braided earlier, but now shabby golden strands hung loosely around her ears and face. *Like a lion,* she thought with sordid amusement. *What I really need is a relaxing bath. Ah, yes. That sounds great!*

Morgan adjusted a couple of her favorite Johnny Mathis records on her old stereo, lit a tiny votive candle, and filled her tub with very warm, scented water. She stripped off her dusty clothes and brushed through her tangled hair, twisting it neatly on top of her head. Sinking slowly into the marvelous, soothing water, she let it lap hungrily around her shoulders and neck.

The sensitive sounds of Mathis, the flickering candlelight, the balmy lilac fragrance, and the refreshing water massaging her gently all served to heal the tumultuous passions that filled her being with turmoil. Here, in her quiet, private domicile, Morgan could forget Grant LeMaster and the ranch and her complicated life.

Was that a door slamming? Morgan listened intently but could only hear the melodious sounds of Mathis singing "Chances Are." She mouthed the familiar words to the cherished old tune, wondering what her chances were of lasting through the summer on the same premises with Grant.

Did she hear voices? Morgan inclined her head toward the door but was serenaded by Mathis's lovely "Small World." She smiled foolishly to herself. *Dummy! You're hearing things! Funny . . .* She hummed along.

She sang softly to herself as she lathered her legs. "Fun-ny, just because de-dum de-dum . . . hummm . . . hummmmmm . . ." Morgan smiled as she hummed the tune, making up self-mocking words here and there. Somehow the singing plus the teasing released her tension. She pushed tepid water around her neck, then stopped . . . sure she heard voices.

She listened, and it was quiet again. There was only one way to find out for certain and that was to climb out of the warm, wonderful tub and investigate! It was probably just her mind playing tricks on her, but just in case . . . Damn! This was yet another annoyance in her evening. Even the solitude of her bath was interrupted! She wrapped herself in a thick towel and, swathed in steam, stepped from the bathroom to her bedroom.

Just as Morgan dropped the concealing towel and reached for

her robe, the door to her room opened! For a split second she was filled with horror, and her mouth opened to utter the scream that filled her mind, but refused to form a sound. Then her brain registered that the man standing in the open doorway, gaping at her nudity, was none other than her husband!

She finally managed, "Grant!"

With suitcases in each hand he stood frozen, ogling in typical male fashion at the curving female shape before him. His gaze steadied, and those penetrating gray eyes darkened with passion as he closed the door with his foot. My God! he thought. She was beautiful! Could he . . . could he actually carry this fakery through for the entire summer? Without touching her? He wanted to sweep her into that bed this very minute . . . He'd never come so close to wanting to force—Oh, god, no! What was he thinking? This was his *wife!* Grant's voice was hoarse as he mumbled, "Sorry, Morgan . . . I shouldn't have barged in like this. . . ." His eyes never left her quivering form.

Hastily Morgan clutched her abandoned shirt to her nude figure. It covered her breasts adequately enough, but not her legs. "What are you doing in here?" she demanded, her voice still shaky from the surprise appearance of a man at her door. But this particular man was now her husband. What did he want of her?

Grant's cool gray eyes claimed her long, bare legs and creamy, uncovered shoulders. A few strands of her long, flaxen hair had worked free from the twist and temptingly reached one shoulder. Her bronze eyes were still wide with fright, only now tinged with the anger—or was it fear—that trembled through her body.

In a slow, well-modulated voice he declared, "Mrs. LeMaster, your husband doesn't sleep in the bunkhouse any longer." He tore his eyes away from her and set one of the suitcases against the wall, then moved toward the closet with the other. It was obvious he had no intention of leaving . . . at least not right away.

Morgan took advantage of the time his back was turned to slip quickly into the shirt and grab her jeans, jerking them furiously over her bare hips. This was no time to bother with underwear. Under the circumstances it was far better to be attired in her discarded work clothes than the flimsy robe. Covering her body also gave her renewed strength to combat this brazen intruder.

81

There was something about being stripped of one's clothes that also tore down defenses. Now Morgan's offensive was powerful. And loud.

"Where the hell do you think you're going? You're *not* sleeping in my room! Get out of here, Grant! Do you hear me? You are not spending the night in *my* room!"

His back was infuriatingly turned to her as he arranged his suit and a couple of clean shirts and jeans in one small corner of the closet. Sarcastically he drawled, "Oh, yes, at that decibel level, Morgan, even the coyotes in the distant San Juans can hear you! Hold it down a little. You'll disturb David."

"David! Where is he?" Involuntarily she glanced toward the door, half expecting the little fellow to saunter in.

Grant's insolent lips curled into a smile. "He's happily settled in the bedroom down the hall. Nice accommodations for a boy. Must have been your brothers' room. David's delighted with the bunk beds and those atrocious cattle horns mounted on the wall—"

Morgan interrupted his insidious rambling. "Grant, don't tell me you've already moved David into this house!" Moving David into the house was a devious act aimed at making Grant's own expulsion more difficult. He was maneuvering her, damn him. And using the child to accomplish his own sordid intent.

Mock surprise aggravated her. "What's wrong, Morgan? You don't mind David using your brothers' old room, do you?"

Caught off guard, she answered, "Well . . . no, but . . ."

"Good," he responded, "because he's all tucked in bed. I'd hate to disturb him now. And you'll be pleased to know that David and I settled our differences before I put him to bed. I apologized for raising my voice and explained where he went wrong. I feel much better, and I'm sure he does, too. Don't you, Morgan?" Amusement played around his rakish eyes.

"Oh, yes, Grant. I'm very relieved. It takes a big man to apologize and especially to inform a six-year-old where he went wrong!" Her sarcastic tone matched his.

A pause in their caustic conversation allowed the soothing tones of Johnny Mathis to filter between them. "What I Did for Love" brought a devilish smile to Grant's countenance. "See, Morgan, even Johnny Mathis understands that some things are done in the name of love. David understands that I scolded him out of my love for him. Surely you can accept that."

Morgan's eyes narrowed. "I doubt that you do anything out of love, Grant. David may believe you, but I don't! And I'm sure he won't mind if you bunk in with him, because you are not sleeping in my room. Now, get out!"

"Not just in your room, my sweet little bride, but in your bed." His voice and quiet and calm, considering his brazen assertion.

"You are not!" Morgan angrily confronted him, hands on her hips, furious with this tall imposing man who came into her room and claimed her bed! No matter that he was her husband! She drew herself up, bitter that she wasn't a little bit taller. Well, she'd show him what a hellcat she could be if he even tried to stay with her!

He faced her boldly. "I am your husband, Morgan. And you are my wife. Mine!"

There was something about his arrogant stance, the square line of his jaw, the unmistakable glow of passion in his eyes that made her want to slap him. As if by a reflex, and without thinking about her actions or their consequences, Morgan raised her arm to hit Grant. But his reflex was even quicker. His large hand flashed up to grasp hers cruelly before it could deliver its stinging blow. Her other hand knotted into a fist and pummeled Grant's shoulder before he grasped it too, capturing both of her hands to prevent the hurt she so desperately wanted to render.

As Morgan wriggled to free herself from the man she hated and so savagely wanted to wound, he held her ever firmly, pinning her arms to her sides and her body to his. The salty smell of his body accosted her senses as he hissed in her face, "Don't ever try to hit me again!"

"You . . . you crude barbarian! You smell like a bear! Let go of me, damn it!" She was surprised—and repulsed—by his controlled assault.

Grant shifted her even closer. "Why? So you can beat me up? Uh-uh. I like this better." And he covered her mouth with his in a vicious, scornful kiss that lacked everything except force.

Morgan had never been kissed—or treated—so roughly before, and she reacted with all the ferocity she could muster against this man who held her brazenly against his taut thighs

83

and insistent masculinity. Her tender lips throbbed from his attack, and still he refused to stop. With her hands held so tightly Morgan's only weapons were her feet, so she began to kick at him. She was oblivious to the fact that her bare feet could render no harm, since he wore his scuffed, leather boots. However her renewed attempts at escape were enough to arouse his anger, and with her arms still pinned, he easily lifted her kicking, squirming body to the bed, where he unceremoniously dumped her.

Morgan was entirely helpless as he covered her protesting, wriggling body with his weight, grasping her legs on either side with his own as he moved over her, making no effort to hide his arousal. His mouth was alarmingly close to hers as he rasped, "Don't think you can overpower me, Morgan! You don't have a chance!"

Morgan was furious! She was being ravaged by her own husband, and who would ever believe her! Through clenched teeth she muttered, "Go ahead, damn you! Rape your wife, and . . . I'll sue you!" As the harsh words left her mouth, angry tears filled her flashing bronze eyes.

Grant's laugh was low and vicious, as he immediately released her hands, leaving them weak and limp. He shifted his body, still trapping her legs with his own, laughing wickedly. "Oh, no, Morgan. I won't force myself on you. You'll have to want me, first," he threatened as he slipped the fingers of one hand just beneath the unsnapped waistband and zipper of her jeans. He traced slow circular patterns, enflaming the sensitive skin of her belly, moving to continue the delicious sensation down the smooth curve of her hip, lingering on her satiny flesh. Morgan steeled herself to what he might do next, fearing her body would betray her resistance. She could feel his fingers gently stroking, gradually decending to her most secret center of desire. Unwillingly she arched toward his searching fingertips, even as she struggled to find words to make him stop.

Morgan's voice trembled with emotion. "So you've proven that you're stronger than me, Grant. What more do you want?"

Passionately he rasped, "You. I want you, Morgan!"

"No! I told you! Grant, you promised! Please . . ."

In the silence that followed Morgan's plea, the Mathis record lulled its sweet tune. "If we only have love . . ."

Grant's voice echoed his remorse. "But we don't, do we, Morgan? There is no love in this marriage. It means nothing that you are my wife. Because there is nothing between us. Nothing . . ." With a low moan he rolled away from her. Sitting on the edge of the bed, Grant cradled his head in his hands. "Oh, God, Morgan. What are we coming to? Can't we have a decent conversation without talking about raping and suing each other? I . . . I don't know what happened to me. I only wanted to talk."

"Talk?" Morgan almost spat at him, scrambling to a sitting position in the middle of the bed. "That's what this is all about? You intrude into my privacy, move your things into my bedroom, and . . . assault me, so we can talk?"

He turned to face her, a crooked smile tugging at his lips as the humor of the situation registered in his passion-crazed mind. "Yeah, something like that." He grinned. "I know it's a little abrupt, but we cowboys lack certain social graces."

The honest expression on his face, the little-boy grin that softened his eyes, the open apology written all over him, brought a reluctant smile to Morgan's face. They both had lost control for a few minutes . . . and they both knew it. "I'll have to admit, you are lacking in social graces, but not in brute strength. I have no doubt that you can break those wild horses out there tomorrow."

Wryly he admitted, "Brute force. But I'm not trying to break wild horses tonight, am I? Just trying to talk to . . . my wife."

Morgan shivered at his words, running her hands over her arms, hugging them unconsciously. "So talk."

Taking a deep, ragged breath, Grant began pacing the floor while he talked. He was still obviously quite shaken by the events of the evening. Or was he simply tormented with unsatisfied desires? "David and I have moved into the ranch house. I won't stay in the bunkhouse any longer."

"When did you decide that?" Morgan was relieved to get some small distance between them.

Instead of answering her question per se, he explained, "After discussing the Rocking M's housing situation with the Simpsons, I know that they like the idea of living in the large bunkhouse.

85

It has the privacy they need, as well as a bath and room for a small kitchen. We can renovate it easily enough for them. Then the smaller bunkhouse can be used for the temporary wranglers that we hire just for the season. The Simpsons do deserve the larger one. Agreed?"

Morgan answered with a sardonic smile. "My, my, aren't you generous! Giving up your nice bedroom to the Simpsons! Why, Grant, how gallant of you!"

"Honestly, Morgan, did you expect to give them the room down the hall and let your husband continue to sleep in the bunkhouse?"

Morgan shrugged with a grin. "Sounds fine to me. That's the way it's been working out so far. Now that you've given up your bunkhouse, where do you expect to live? Here?" She folded her arms across her breast.

Grant matched her action, but looked ever so masculine with his wide stance and gray eyes glaring into her. "David is settled down the hall, and I intend to live with my wife."

Morgan's brown eyes narrowed at him. "Grant, we agreed . . ."

"I know what we agreed. And regardless of what happened tonight I promise there'll be no more . . . brute force. I'll set up my office in the little room next door and sleep in there. No one will know it but you and me. Does that satisfy you?"

She agreed, somewhat skeptically. "Looks like you have it all figured out."

"What I didn't figure on was what happened tonight." His voice was suddenly low and gentle. "Morgan, look at me. I'm . . . I'm sorry about what happened. I didn't intend to lose control like that."

Morgan blinked and looked down. "I guess I lost a little control, too, Grant. I pushed you . . ."

"Let's let it drop. I . . . I'll just get clean clothes and use the shower down the hall. I have a big day tomorrow. Boyd and Willa are moving in, and I intend to ride at least one of those wild horses." Grant moved quietly to the closet and took the clothes he needed, then left her alone without glancing back.

Morgan sat curled up on the bed for long, lonely moments. For some strange reason she felt very sad and mixed up after

86

Grant left her. She could hear him moving about the room next to hers and wondered what he was doing. Then she rebuffed herself for even caring. Deep down she feared her own feelings toward this steely man who had just left her bedroom. He had excited her with his touch, even though their meeting had been stimulated by anger. It wasn't his anger that excited her. It was his eyes and the smoldering emotions hidden there. She longed to feel his arms around her again and his lips on hers. But gently this time. She didn't want to feel his angry, punishing lips ever again. Yet, according to his promise, she wouldn't feel his lips again . . . unless she desired it. At that thought she tenderly touched her bruised lips, knowing she desired Grant very much.

As Johnny Mathis crooned soft lyrics of forever-after love, Morgan wondered if it could possibly be love she felt, or just desire.

CHAPTER SIX

By ten the next day Willa and Boyd Simpson were moving into Grant and his son's ex-bedroom. As soon as their things were unloaded from the small pickup truck, Grant and Boyd went off together to see about the horses and start their day's work. Morgan stayed with Willa, trying to make the rugged old bunkhouse look like a home for a woman.

"I found these curtains in the back closet, Willa. They should fit the windows." Morgan unfolded the chintz material for Willa's inspection. "How do they look?"

"Yes, I think they'll do fine." Willa beamed at the feminine addition to the rather barren room. "When we get curtain rods . . ."

"I have everything we need right here." Morgan motioned to some equipment she had left near the door. "I'll put them up while you finish unpacking."

"Thank you, Mrs. LeMaster. But I can do that if you have more important things to do."

Morgan pulled a chair over to the window and stood on it to align the rod correctly. "Right now the most important thing I have to do is to make sure you and Boyd are settled and comfortable. And please, Willa, call me Morgan. I want you to be my friend as well as Grant's. As closely as we'll all be working and living, first names will be much easier."

Willa smiled amiably. She had a beautiful smile and a lively twinkle in her blue eyes that spoke of a gayness that still pervaded her spirit. And Morgan liked that. *Yes,* she thought. *We'll get along fine.*

Willa halted and assessed Morgan honestly. "You know, Morgan, you and Grant seem to be an ideal couple. I think he made a real good choice for a wife."

Morgan couldn't hide her mirth at what Willa had intended as a compliment. Wouldn't she be surprised at the "ideal couple" if she knew Morgan had done the choosing? "Thanks, Willa, but you know I wasn't actually his first choice. Grant was married first to an Indian woman. She was David's mother." Morgan felt it best to get the facts about David's parentage out in the open at the beginning. Of course Willa probably knew Grant's first wife, or knew about her.

Willa cast a puzzled glance at Morgan, who busily hammered the curtain rod in place. "No," she said thoughtfully, "I didn't know her. But it seems he said something about you being newlyweds the day you stopped by to hire us."

"Yes," Morgan agreed, silently amused at the term *newlyweds.* It hardly described their status. "In fact, the wedding was just last week." She stood back to see if the curtains hung evenly.

"Then you're still on your honeymoon!" Willa exclaimed, delighted with the romantic notion. "Now if there's ever a time that you and Grant want some privacy—you know—just give me the word. Boyd and I'll see that little David is completely entertained."

Morgan's fair complexion colored immediately at Willa's bold suggestion. "Oh . . . uh, thanks," she mumbled. *Honeymoon, indeed!*

"I didn't mean to embarrass you, honey." Willa chuckled knowingly. "But I was a newlywed once myself, and I remember. It must be difficult to marry and become an instant mother. And I know it's inconvenient to have us around the ranch all the time."

Morgan answered stiffly, "Actually, Willa, our main concern is to get this ranch running smoothly this summer. And you and Boyd were hired with that purpose in mind."

"Oh, I didn't mean to interfere . . ."

Morgan smiled tightly. "You didn't, Willa. But we all have

89

lots of work to do before July fourth. Now would you like to see the house and the rest of the ranch?"

The older woman nodded. "I especially want to see the kitchen. Grant made such a point of making sure I could cook, I'd like to see the place where I'm to do it." Willa was slender and rather lithesome. She and her husband were in their late fifties and both emitted a calm strength, a cohesiveness that had enabled them to remain serene and happy through life.

Morgan led the way to the kitchen and thought with an inward smile how this steadfast couple resembled each other—just a little—as many couples seem to do who live together for a long time. She wondered if she and Grant would . . . but no. There wouldn't be time for that. They wouldn't be together very long . . . only one summer.

Morgan stepped to the back door and indicated for Willa to precede her. "Here it is, Willa. The most important room in the house! At least the men around here think so!" Both women giggled in agreement about the importance of a full plate of appetizing food to a contented ranch hand. Morgan eagerly confessed that she was only too glad to relinquish that responsibility to Willa. The uncomfortable tension of moments before was behind them.

Hereafter Willa would be careful to skirt the sensitive issues of Morgan's marriage and motherhood. Otherwise they would get along fine.

They examined the kitchen and toured the house, then the women walked toward the barns. They ended up at the corral fence where they watched Boyd and Grant tending to one of the horses. Both men were intense, working to adjust the saddle, stirrups, and reins. Suddenly Grant lifted his boot to the stirrup and heaved himself smartly into the saddle. Boyd moved back quickly, stumbling against the fence in his haste. And the big horse on which Grant perched went crazy! He jumped and hopped stiff-legged, twisted, turned, galloped a stretch, then stopped on a dime and whipped around in a circle. It was that last circle that got Grant.

Morgan watched, horrified, as Grant flew through the air, almost in slow motion, and landed with a thud on the hard earth. A masculine voice hurled angry expletives through the air, then all was quiet as everyone strained to know the fate of the Rocking M's newest bronc rider. Dust filled her nostrils before Morgan realized that she had scaled the fence and entered the corral at a dead run. As she reached Grant, his gray eyes gazed up foggily into hers. He stared for a moment, as if wondering who she was . . . or, more likely, what she was doing there.

"Are . . . are you all right, Grant?" she questioned breathlessly.

He nodded abruptly and started to get up. Involuntarily she reached for him, not actually helping, just gripping his arm reassuringly. His muscles tightened under her clasp.

Boyd's shout interrupted the moment. "Come on, Grant. You've got to mount him again! You can't let him go free after this. You've got to break him, son!"

Grant broke away from her, as if mesmerized by Boyd's voice. Morgan could hear him muttering, "I'll take him even if I break every goddamn bone in my body . . . I can do it!" Boyd shouted at her to get out of the way and Morgan quickly obeyed, clambering to the top of the fence rail near where Willa stood. Boyd was right, of course. Grant had to show the animal who was boss, who was superior. He had to ride the horse, too, for his own self-esteem. Morgan knew it had to be done. And yet she also knew the pain her husband was enduring. She had seen the dullness of his eyes and knew he was hurting. Flinching with each jolt of Grant's body, gasping every time his frame swayed in the saddle, Morgan mentally suffered the ride along with Grant. Finally, when both the man and horse were swathed in great sweaty lather, the animal stopped jumping. He stood stockstill for a few seconds, heaving, during which time Grant gathered his strength for another onslaught.

But Boyd shouted triumphantly, "Whoopee! He's done, Grant! Finished! You did it! Now walk him around. Just keep him moving for a while."

Grant did as Boyd instructed, and Morgan breathed a sigh of relief . . . proud as hell of Grant. Yet a niggling thought inside her refused to withdraw. Their alliance had placed Grant in the hazardous position of breaking those horses . . . or else. And he was too stubborn to quit. Morgan knew that breaking horses was always risky, even for experts. Grant could have been crippled . . . or killed . . . because of her!

She knocked faintly on his door, not wishing to disturb him if he was already asleep. A groaning mumble answered her knock and Morgan opened the door slowly, saying, "It's me, Grant. I . . . have something for you. For your back." She eased into the darkened room where he lay, half stretched out on the narrow bed. At one time this had been her room, and she had slept on this very bed on which Grant tried to make his lengthy body fit. He sprawled with one knee bent and one arm flung over his eyes, and he looked . . . oh, so very masculine lying there.

He didn't move, but verbally acknowledged her presence with barely a civil, "What do you want?"

Morgan swallowed hard as her eyes accustomed themselves to the darkness. She could see his angular form more clearly now. He wore no shirt to hide dark, curly hair that spread across his chest, trailed his flat belly, and ended in an enticing line beneath his shorts. The sight of his virility thrilled her, awakening bold desires that had never been stirred. *Not even with André.*

"Grant? Maybe this will help." Morgan was suddenly timid before him. She wanted to touch him, and yet . . .

Grant moved his arm upward a little, so that he could see her. It was hard to believe this shy form standing nearby was the same little hellcat he wrestled to the bed only the night before. She was like an apparition, with her golden hair flowing over the shoulders of a pale dressing gown. Her dark eyes were so serious . . . oh, God! She was so beautiful! "Morgan?" It was a question, as if he could hardly believe it was her. "What—"

"Well, who else? Come on. Sit up. Drink this. It'll help you relax." She handed him a small glass.

He reached for it, rough fingers touching hers in the process. "What is it?" He raised his body with a groan and gave her a curious glance.

Sighing, Morgan joined him on the bed, sitting cautiously on the edge. "This is what's left of the champagne. I . . . thought you might like some tonight. It's all we have in the house right now. I suppose a stiff shot of whiskey would suit you better, but—"

He interrupted abruptly. "This is fine. Thanks."

"How do you feel?" She watched him gulp the drink.

He looked at her solemnly, his ashen eyes tired and dull. "Like hell."

She nodded, as if knowing that would be his answer. "Finish your drink, then turn over. I'll rub your back with this deep-heating stuff. Willa loaned it to us. She says it's the best for aching muscles."

Grant eyed her closely. "Am I dreaming, Morgan? You graciously bring me a drink . . . and now you're offering to rub my aching back?"

She nodded with a sheepish smile. "I guess I've got a bad case of the guilts, Grant. I'm . . . I'm sorry I put you in this situation of having to break those two wild horses. I just realized today how very dangerous it is. And I know you didn't bargain for that when you—"

With a loud groan he stretched out on his belly. "I didn't bargain for a lot of things, Morgan. But then neither did you. I just chalk this one up to experience. One down and one more to go! While I've got you here, and you're in a sympathetic mood, let's try Willa's remedy. What are you waiting for?"

Morgan looked at the broad, sinewy back before her and began to touch him gingerly. His muscles were tense and hard, coiling tighter as she ran her slim hands over him. Lightly at first, she covered his muscular back with the menthol-fragrant ointment, then moved to retrace the taut expanse of masculinity with more ardor. When he obviously flinched at her touch, she asked apprehensively, "Did I hurt you?"

A rough laugh escaped his lips. "You didn't, Morgan. But that damn horse certainly did his share. Ahhh, my arms feel like they've been pulled from their sockets. But don't stop. Right there, Morgan . . . ooooh, that's nice, honey . . ." His voice was almost a guttural groan.

Morgan proceeded to do as he instructed, kneading his shoulders, massaging his well-knit forearms, manipulating the cords that led from his backbone around his ribs. She enjoyed the task, reacting easily to the warmth created between her manipulating hands and his tight-muscled body. The ointment seemed to create a magnetic field, attracting her to his radiating appeal.

"There, how's that? Feel better?" Morgan murmured.

"Ummm, yes." He sighed, shifting to a more comfortable position. "Don't stop, Morgan. This almost makes me glad I married you."

"Almost?"

"Um-hum," he mumbled.

She continued to massage him deliberately, smiling to herself at his teasing jab at their marriage. Last night she would have taken offense. But tonight, after seeing the risks he took today— for her and the ranch—she knew that she was asking a tremendous amount of him. Perhaps too much. "Grant . . ."

"Hummm?"

"I'm sorry about the deal with the wild horses. I . . . I think it's too much to expect you to break another one. You're right. This wasn't in the bargain . . . and I shouldn't ask it of you."

"You getting soft, Morgan? We haven't even tried Blue Velvet yet. He's tomorrow."

Morgan's voice was urgent. "No, Grant. Please . . . don't ride again tomorrow. Rest for a few days."

"Tomorrow's the day, honey. I'll ride him or . . ." His words dwindled toward the end and were unintelligible.

Morgan leaned forward trying to catch his words and failed to notice the relaxed nature of the taut muscles which she had massaged into submission.

"Grant, I can't let you ride again tomorrow. I just didn't think about how dangerous breaking horses can be . . . especially for a relative novice. Not that you're . . . well, you were pretty good today, Grant. But I can't let you take that risk again. In fact, I want to sell Blue Velvet. And from now on we'll buy horses that are already broken. That's what we'll do. We need some pack horses or mules, anyway. Maybe we can strike a trade. I . . . just don't want to risk . . . my husband . . . with those wild horses again. Why, if anything ever happened to you, Grant, and you were injured, I'd never forgive myself." She paused, amazed by her own admissions. "Grant?" She halted and leaned closer, listening to his steady breathing. Grant was asleep and hadn't heard a thing she'd said.

Morgan sighed and stood up, surveying the prone man who slept so soundly before her. One of his legs sprawled across the

94

bed, the other hung half off the side. He looked so damned uncomfortable, she wondered if she should wake him and . . . what? Offer him her bed? She acknowledged that he would be able to rest better. But would she? Could she possibly think of sleeping next to him? My God, she could hardly stand to look at him now! Quickly she turned away from his appealing virility and retreated from the room, frustrated, puzzled, bedeviled by the man she called her husband.

The next morning, true to her promise, Willa cheerfully prepared breakfast for everyone. In fact, by the time Morgan stumbled in, the men had finished and already left for work.

"They're repairing that blue devil's stall this morning," offered Willa.

Morgan stirred her coffee absently. "Repairing a stall? What's wrong with it?"

Willa poured herself a cup of coffee and joined Morgan at the table. She chatted happily, omitting the answers Morgan sought. "My, my, how that bunch can eat! Do you know that little David ate five pancakes! And Grant—"

"You fixed pancakes for breakfast this morning? Well, no wonder they're all so happy with your cooking, Willa! I've never served pancakes in the morning. They must think they're in heaven!" Morgan laughed. "That's just something I can't face so early in the morning. Boy, am I glad you're here."

Willa reached over and patted the younger woman's hand. "Not nearly as glad as I am to be here, Morgan. Boyd and I are real honored that you and Grant decided to hire us. There aren't many people willing to do that nowadays."

Morgan smiled easily across the table. "Well, the feelings are mutual, Willa. We need your help to make this ranch work. Now what's wrong with the stall? I know it was fine yesterday."

Willa shook her head in dismay. "That blue devil of a horse kicked the walls down during the night. He made a huge hole in it and, if he'd had more time, would have knocked the whole stall down! That one's a bad animal."

Morgan shrugged. "Well, maybe it'll keep them busy today and they won't try to break him. I'm going to sell him as soon as I can. Blue Velvet . . . he has such a beautiful name. Why can't he live up to it?"

Willa chuckled. "Oh, he lives up to his name, all right. You know what the rodeo bronc riders say about a horse with *velvet* in its name. . . ."

Morgan looked up curiously. "No, what?"

Willa sipped her coffee before answering. "It's the meanest horses that get the name *Velvet.*"

Morgan frowned. "Couldn't be meaner than that one yesterday!"

"Oh, sure." Willa shrugged. "That one Grant rode yesterday was a pussycat compared to some. I remember one time on a ranch out in Montana. I was very young, mind you. But there was an Appaloosa stallion named Calico Velvet that nobody could ride. Boyd was breaking horses every day and had tried that spotted devil three days in a row . . . and three times had been bucked off! On the fourth day I got it in my head that I could ride that horse. So I saddled him and, oh, he stood so still. I thought he was gentled by all the riding of the past few days, but he sure fooled me! As soon as I touched that saddle, he jumped higher and longer and rounder than he ever had . . . at least, it felt like he did! But I stayed on him and by the end of the ride, that horse walked me around the corral and all the hands—the men—gathered on the fence rails and applauded! Gosh, those days were long ago!" A happy glimmer lit Willa's blue eyes as she recalled that glorious day in her past.

Morgan smiled warmly. "Willa, that's a beautiful story. I'll bet Boyd was proud of you!"

"Proud?" Willa scoffed. "He was madder'n a wet hen! Didn't speak to me for two days! Said I could have killed myself!" She shook her head as she rose and finished cleaning up the dishes.

Morgan's finger ran slowly around the rim of her cup. The reason for Boyd's anger at Willa echoed in her mind and she shuddered at the thought. Grant could have gotten himself killed yesterday on that horse. And it would have been all her fault. *All her fault.*

Willa's laugh interrupted Morgan's morbid thoughts. "You know something, Morgan? Boyd wouldn't admit he was proud of me, but he was. I could see it in his face. But I guess the most important thing was that *I* was proud of me! I'll never forget that day!"

"Well, I'm proud of you, too, Willa!" Morgan stated emphatically. Suddenly her attention was turned to the far corral. The blue-gray stallion was prancing and pawing, under the guidance of Boyd, followed closely by Grant. She stood up with a start, her voice shrill and nearly wild. "My God, Willa! They're going to ride him! They're going to ride Blue Velvet! Grant—"

Willa's gaze followed Morgan's, but her tone was quite nonchalant. "I'm not surprised. There's one thing cowboys don't tolerate, and that's to be bested by an animal. The sooner they break him, the better."

"Oh, no! He can't! He just can't!" Like a flash Morgan bolted out the door, running at top speed the distance to the far corral. In the time it took her to reach it, Grant was already astride the huge horse. Gasping for breath, Morgan gripped the fence rail and watched the dreadful sight of Grant clinging desperately to the wildly bucking animal. He hung on for long, agonizing moments of hell until—inevitably—he flew through the air once again. The landing was accompanied by loud curses, however, and he was on his feet, brushing the dust from his seat by the time Morgan could race to his side.

"Grant! Are you all right?"

He turned his steel-hard eyes on her sharply. "Morgan, get out of this corral! Leave me alone! I'm fine!"

Hurt and astonishment filled her heart at his words, and she sought a quick reason for standing beside him in the dusty corral. "I . . . I want to ride him next, Grant! It's my turn to try Blue Velvet!" Morgan couldn't believe her own voice. She had never ridden more than a very slow gelding in her life. And here she wanted to mount a wild stallion!

Grant waved her away. "Are you crazy? No, Morgan, I'll take him. He's much too dangerous for you."

The belittling remark in itself was enough to spark Morgan's vengeful spirit. But it also served as a reminder of the reason this horse had the name of Blue Velvet. "The meanest horses get the name of Velvet." Morgan was crazy with the thought of Grant riding this insanely wild horse . . . and getting hurt. A terrible knot clamped viciously in the pit of her stomach, choking her with fear and blocking out all reasonable thought. As Grant bent to retrieve his hat, Morgan moved past him. Reaching the spot where Boyd held the impatient horse, she ordered firmly, "Hold him still for me, Boyd."

Before Boyd or Grant realized what she was doing, Morgan had mounted the angry, feisty animal. As soon as her weight hit the saddle, Blue Velvet bolted free from Boyd's startled grasp and began his stiff-legged stint across the entire corral. He turned and twisted and jumped while Morgan held on gamely, her flaxen hair flying wildly and her small body jostling like a puppet.

Grant watched, astounded, consternation paralyzing him where he stood in the center of the corral. He didn't have long to wait for the gruesome sight of Morgan—his wife—hurtling over the bowed head of the devil horse and landing in a still, unceremonious heap in the dust. He wasn't even aware of his own hoarse voice repeatedly yelling her name as he raced across the dry earth to kneel over Morgan's unmoving form.

CHAPTER SEVEN

The balding doctor looked over gold, wire-rimmed bifocals at Grant. "Mr. LeMaster, the X rays show your wife has two broken ribs. She'll be in a lot of pain for the next few days. Her concussion is mild, but she'll need complete bed rest for at least a week, maybe two. Now we could hospitalize her, but if you think she can get the rest she needs at home—"

"Oh, yes, Doctor. I'll make sure of it. Complete bed rest." His eyes caressed Morgan, who lay very still on the examining table with her eyes closed. "We have an excellent housekeeper who'll help me take care of her. And I'll see that she stays in bed."

At that statement Morgan's eyes flickered open to give Grant a hard stare. But she said nothing.

The old doctor raised his eyebrows knowingly and laid an experienced hand on Grant's arm. In a lowered voice he advised, "And you must be very careful with your wife, Mr. LeMaster. She—uh—those ribs will be terribly sore for several weeks. You'll have to help her keep them wrapped with the Ace bandage and you may need to tighten or loosen it, as her pain dictates. She'll let you know, I'm sure."

Grant nodded seriously and winked at Morgan, who was in too much pain to see the humor in his response. "I'm sure she will. And I'll keep my distance, Doctor, believe me."

Grant assisted Morgan to her feet and wrapped a strong, secure arm around her as they walked slowly out to his roomy

99

Suburban. "Do you want to lay down in the back, Morgan? I can move the seat easily."

She shook her head. "Just help me into the front seat. I'd rather sit. Getting up and down is worse than staying up after I'm already here."

"Sure, Morgan." He settled her in the seat and drove very carefully back to the ranch. There she was greeted by a very anxious trio. Little David was curious and concerned, as was Boyd Simpson. But obviously the most upset was Willa. She hovered like a little hen, settling Morgan comfortably in the newly made bed.

"How about hot tea, Morgan? Does that sound good?"

Morgan nodded with a tight smile, just to please the older woman. She closed her eyes, and Grant followed Willa out of the bedroom. Outside, in the hallway, Morgan could hear their terse exchange.

Grant's voice rumbled. "Willa, she's very lucky. Just a couple of broken ribs and a very mild concussion. Doctor says she needs complete bed rest. Can you help me make sure that she gets it?"

"Oh, yes, I'll see to it, Grant. I'll take good care of her. It's the least I can do."

"I knew you would, Willa. That's why I didn't put her in the hospital. I figured we could keep a better eye on her here. I don't know what got into her. Why in hell would she tackle that wild horse?"

Willa's timbre-filled voice answered. "I'm afraid I put the notion in her head, Grant. It's all my fault."

"Your fault, Willa? How's that?"

"Oh, I told her about the time I rode a bronc in Montana. I'm sure she thought she could do it, too. I'm awfully sorry. I sure didn't mean to suggest something so dangerous to her."

Grant's voice was soothing as they walked away. "Now, Willa, I don't think you influenced her. That girl has a mind of her own. . . . I'm sure it was her own crazy idea. You are definitely not to blame. . . ."

Their voices floated away until Morgan was awakened by a male voice that rumbled near her. "Morgan, would you like to sip this hot tea Willa has made?"

She forced herself to wake up, moving painfully so that she

100

could sip the hot drink. "Yes, that feels good inside." She smiled up at her worried husband.

The concerned look on his face set his jaw firmly and increased the intensity of his deep-set gray eyes. His rough hand brushed her face—an involuntary move of affection and care.

"Hey," she coaxed. "Don't look so down. I'm okay. Just need a little rest."

He nodded. "Yes, I know. And here's your medicine. Doctor says it'll help you relax."

She gulped the capsule obediently, since she was in no position to resist Grant's wishes this time. "It'll put me to sleep, you mean. I . . . I want you to know something, Grant. Tell Willa—"

His hand pushed on her shoulder, settling her flat against the bed. "Not now, Morgan. You need to rest. We can talk later."

"Now!" Morgan's voice rose in defiance. "I want to talk now! Tell her it wasn't her fault at all. It was all my idea. I . . . I just didn't want you . . . you to get . . . hurt."

"Me?" he asked incredibly. "But, Morgan—why?"

She smiled weakly. "This could be you lying here, Grant. Or worse. And I'd never forgive myself. . . ."

"Oh, God, Morgan. You didn't . . . for me?"

Her eyes closed involuntarily and squeezed two tears out of the corners onto pale cheeks. She barely felt his lips kiss them away and couldn't decipher his mumbled, "Now, I've got to live with the guilt, little one."

The remainder of that day was a fog in Morgan's memory. She floated in and out of wakefulness, only aware of one face visible every time she awoke. The serious, concerned image of her husband filled her mind—she thought she was dreaming of him but he was real and didn't leave her side all day.

By nightfall Morgan rallied enough to sip rich, fragrant broth lovingly prepared by Willa. Grant eagerly helped her eat. Afterward he assisted as she hobbled to the bathroom.

Finally in a weak voice she called for him. "Grant?"

Outside the closed door he answered, "Yes? Do you need . . . help?" There was a helplessness to his tone.

"Would you hand me my robe? It's hanging just inside the closet."

"Sure." In a moment a masculine hand eased the bathroom

door open just enough to squeeze the blue satiny robe inside. "Do you want your nightgown?"

After a pause she answered, "No, I don't think I could get it over my head. This will be fine because I can just slip it on, if only . . ."

"What? Should I get Willa?"

Morgan refrained from the laughter that welled up inside her, knowing that it would hurt those ribs. But there was definite amusement in her answer. "Now, how would that look, Mr. LeMaster? 'Hey, Willa, would you come help my wife undress? I've never seen her like that!' "

His answer was quick and pointed. "But I have."

Morgan sighed in exasperation, not able to accomplish her painful task of stripping off the tight jeans she still wore. In frustration she gasped, "Then come in here and help me. You're my husband!"

Without hesitation the door opened and Grant stood there in all his glory, trying not to gape at her, feeling suddenly restrained.

Morgan ignored the expression on his taut face as she explained in a persistent voice, "All I need is for you to pull these jeans off my hips. I just can't bend over to get them down." She had shed her blouse and donned the robe, which clung seductively to her firm-nippled breasts.

Grant reached for her waist where the jeans were already unsnapped and unzipped, but continued to rest snuggly against her hips. Gently he tried to budge the skintight garment, averting his eyes from those prominent breasts, which lay just at eye level. "They're tight!"

"I know that! That's why I couldn't get them off! Pull harder, Grant! Come on! I can't believe you're suddenly bashful!"

His eyes darted to her face, as he rumbled, "Bashful is not my problem, Morgan, and you damn well know it!" Inserting his long fingers around the snug waistband, he firmly pushed the jeans over her hips, allowing his hands to trail her hips and legs as he removed the offending garment. Dropping the stiff denim pants on the floor, Grant stood before her, drinking in her half-clad body with hungry eyes. Her bikini panties had rolled into a narrow item that hid nothing as his eyes rested momentarily

102

on her V patch before traveling upward to her breasts, then on to her large, brown eyes. As he looked deeply into them, Morgan watched a small muscle flex in his cheek, while his hands sought her.

Gently caressing her breasts, his thumbs circled the ripe nipples. Then his hands groped for the robe which hung openly inviting, barely revealing her tightly wrapped rib cage, reminding him of her injury. "My God, Morgan!" he admonished raggedly. "Cover yourself! How much do you think I can stand?"

Her wide eyes were not entirely innocent. "I . . . I didn't think about it, Grant. You know what the doctor said."

Tiny beads of perspiration lined his upper lip. "To hell with what the doctor says. I'm waiting on word from you."

Her eyes fogged with pain and she shook her head. "Please, Grant . . . help me back to bed."

With strained control he helped her across the room. When she was settled comfortably, he mumbled good night and hurriedly left the room. Morgan drifted to sleep to the unmistakable sound of the shower down the hall. Her dreams were vivid and numerous, alternating from running in the rain she thought she heard, to her wild ride on the devil horse. Round and round she went, up and down, jerking from side to side until she was again flying through the air! *No! Oh, no!* It was Grant flying across the sky! Grant was falling! Her own distraught screams woke her, and Morgan clutched frantically at the alarmed man near her, amid frenzied cries of "Grant! Grant, hold me!"

"It's okay, Morgan. I'm here," he soothed, caressing her perspiration-drenched forehead and rumpled hair.

"Grant? Are you really here? Are you all right?" She held him tightly, listening to his strong heartbeat and absorbing the secure warmth from his body.

"I'm fine, little one. You must have been dreaming." His hands were strong and reassuring on her.

"Oh, God, the dreams were awful! Hold me, Grant. Don't leave me, please. Just hold me tonight," she pleaded.

His powerful arms locked comfortably around her trembling body and he murmured, "I won't leave you, little one. I'm here whenever you need me." And he stayed with her the remainder of the night, reassuring her occasionally, caressing her when she cried out, loving her with gentle promises. She wanted him . . . needed him . . . had cried out for him. She clung to him now in her pain, but would she want his touch in the clear light of day when her pain subsided? Grant LeMaster spent the night in the glory of his wife's arms, but there was little sleep for him during the long, dark hours.

David's happy, young voice bolstered her even before his small, dark face appeared in the doorway of Morgan's bedroom. "I have something for you, Morgan. I made a picture for you!"

"Well, great! Let me see it!" Morgan had been plagued with headaches all week and this was the first day Grant and Willa had allowed David to visit.

"Too loud," they had said.

But Morgan had missed the youngest member of her little family and was delighted to see him now. She smiled teasingly and begged, "Give me a hug, David. I've really missed you this week. What have you been up to?"

He wrapped his small arms around her neck and hugged her tightly. He clung for only a brief second, but long enough for Morgan to realize that he sought her love. It was the first time she knew—*really knew*—that she was more to David than just an acquaintance of Grant's. Unexpected tears of joy sprang to her eyes as the small boy slipped away and exclaimed eagerly, "I've missed you, too, Morgan. We haven't done nothing fun all week. I haven't had any ice cream in a whole week! It's just no fun around here without you!"

Morgan frowned seriously, and gave Grant a disparaging glance. "No ice cream at all? How awful, David! We'll have to do something about that! I'm ready for some pistachio! How about you?"

David thought solemnly for a moment. "Rocky Road is still my favorite."

"That kid knows what he likes and he sticks with it!" laughed Grant from where he leaned against the doorjamb. He folded his arms across his chest and an expression of pure pleasure lit his face for the first time that week. David was definitely good for Morgan and he probably should have let him visit her sooner.

104

"I want to see the picture, David," Morgan encouraged.

Timidly the child held the paper up for her perusal. "See? You're not the only one who fell off Blue Velvet."

Morgan gazed curiously at the stick figures displayed on the paper. "I know this is Blue Velvet in the center, but who's this?" she asked, pointing.

"That's Grant!" he announced proudly. "See his big hat over here on the ground?"

Stiffly she nodded. "Grant rode Blue Velvet?"

"Yep." David smiled majestically at Grant, who suddenly seemed to cringe in the doorway. "And he broke him, too. Took all day, but he finally rode him!"

"Grant?" Morgan's voice rose in alarm as she looked to her husband for confirmation.

Grant shrugged with a meek smile. "Out of the mouths of babes."

Morgan looked back at David's innocent face. "I love the picture, David. I'll put it up on the wall, so I can see it every day. And you are a very fine artist!" She smiled warmly and pulled him closer for a quick kiss on his tanned cheek.

Grant stepped forward to end the visit. His little son had already revealed more than he wanted Morgan to know. "You'd better run along now, David. I think Morgan needs her . . . uh, her rest. This is about all the excitement she needs in one day."

"Okay. See you later, Morgan. Don't forget about the ice cream!" David smiled happily before skipping out of the room.

Morgan faced Grant angrily, her voice shaking with anticipation. "Grant, was he telling the truth? Did you ride that . . . *that horse* this week?"

He stood near the bed, hands on his hips. "My son doesn't lie."

She looked away from his steady gaze. "Grant, how could you? I told you I want to sell Blue Velvet. I don't want to take a chance of anyone else getting hurt on him. What if you'd been . . . what if . . ."

He sat on the edge of the bed and took her hand. "But I'm fine. Just a little sore, that's all. Don't you understand, Morgan? I had to conquer him, especially after he threw you. I just had to."

Her brown eyes filled with tears. "I don't want that horse

105

around here. And I don't want you to ride him anymore, Grant. You did all this while I was sleeping my life away. I would never have known. . . ."

He kissed her palm tenderly. "I appreciate your concern, Morgan. I've missed you this week, little one. There was no one to rub my aching back at night—"

Pink colored her cheeks and she smiled involuntarily through her tears. "Oh, Grant—" Morgan's arms encircled his neck, pulling him down to her waiting lips. Tenderly, passionately, his mouth caressed hers, trailing along her cheeks and licking away the tears. He then moved down her sensitive neck to the wildly pulsating hollow of her throat, murmuring, "Oh, God, you're warm and inviting in that bed, Morgan."

"And I can smell you've been working hard all day." Morgan giggled, wrinkling her nose at him.

Just as Grant's mouth covered hers again, hungrily seeking her delectable sweetness, Willa cleared her throat from the doorway and announced, "Supper will be ready in half an hour. Don't you dare hurt her ribs after all she's been through this week, Grant LeMaster!"

Grant stood clumsily, like a little boy caught with his hand in the cookie jar. He turned steely eyes to the older woman. "I can kiss my wife without injuring her, Willa!" He then turned and stalked out, leaving the two women alone.

Willa ignored his remark and continued talking with Morgan as if Grant had never been there. "Do you feel like having something solid to eat tonight, Morgan honey? I made some chicken soup for you."

"That sounds great, Willa. And I'm starved!" Morgan smiled enthusiastically. "Gosh, I'm glad you were here this week. What would we have done without you?"

Wistfully Willa said, "Without me you probably wouldn't even have tried to ride that devil horse."

"Now that's not true, Willa. I . . . it was my own idea. I'll agree, it was a foolish one but I have to take full credit for it. I . . . I just didn't want Grant to get hurt. He's not a real cowboy, you know. He's just doing all this for . . . to save the ranch." She couldn't bring herself to say he was working for her. Or was he? Hope sprang in her heart at the thought.

Willa raised her eyebrows. "Grant LeMaster can take care of himself, and he's more of a roughneck than you think. I know one thing, though. He'd do anything for you, Morgan. Well, I gotta get to my supper. I'll bring your soup in a few minutes."

After supper Morgan lay awake, pondering Willa's earlier statements and listening to the evening sounds of the family. The men went back outside for some late chores, and she could hear Willa clanking about the kitchen. Then Grant helped David with his bath and getting ready for bed. A good-night kiss from the little boy was the only contact she had all evening with the family. They were already functioning very well without her. Nothing was more miserable than to lay helplessly and listen to others' activities, knowing they really didn't need you.

Grant poked his head into her room with a large towel drapped over his bare shoulders. "Do you need anything before I take my shower, Morgan?"

Her eyes lit up and she responded eagerly, "That sounds like a great idea, Grant. I'd like to take a bath!"

He looked at her sharply. "I think you should wait, Morgan. This is the first afternoon you've felt decent."

"All right, a shower then. It's been days since I've touched water! And I want a shower tonight. I think it'll make me feel much better. Come on, Grant. Help me up."

Reluctantly Grant approached her. "Morgan, I don't think you should be in the shower alone."

She laughed and threw back the covers. "What do you suggest? Want to go in there with me?"

"Don't tempt me, little one!"

She reached up, and he pulled her stiffly to her feet. It was an awkward movement, but it was the only way she could raise up without pain. She squeezed his hands. "I'll be fine, Grant. Just stay close by."

He stood helplessly as she gingerly made her way into the bathroom. Once again this little spitfire of a willful bride was getting her way. "Morgan, you aren't feeling dizzy, are you? Will you call me if you feel the least bit sick? If you lost your balance in the shower, you could be seriously hurt."

She smiled seductively at him. "Would you come in and get me if I called?"

His expressive eyes answered even before he assured her, "You bet!"

"I need this shower, Grant. I'll feel much better afterward. You'll see!" she promised and closed the bathroom door behind her.

Heaving a sigh, Grant sat on the edge of the bed, waiting impatiently until she finished. Oh, how he wanted to burst into that little room and take her. After all, she was his wife, and she had tempted him on more than one occasion—but he had promised. Damn! Why had he promised?

A few minutes later Morgan emerged slowly from the steamy bathroom, a glorious smile on her flushed face. She had tied the blue satiny robe loosely around her waist, and it clung to her still-damp breasts, outlining the prominent nipples. Her long hair was wet and dripped dark spots around the shoulders of the robe . . . and lower. Oh, God—how he wanted to jerk that robe away!

"I feel wonderful and . . . clean." She beamed. "Thanks for waiting, Grant. Now you go ahead and take your shower. I'm going to sit right here and dry my hair."

He hovered nervously, helping her to ease into the chair, plugging in the hair dryer. "How do you feel? Are you sure you'll be okay while I'm gone?"

She nodded, not aware of just how sensuous she looked with her face freshly scrubbed and that thin robe clinging seductively around her shapely body.

Grant turned away quickly, stepped into the shower, and adjusted the temperature to cool. By the time he emerged, shirtless and wearing casual shorts, Morgan was struggling to dry the long ends of her blond hair.

"I can't seem to reach all of it without hurting my ribs," she complained, offering him just the invitation he needed.

"Here, let me," he accepted willingly. He dried, burrowed, caressed the lengthy flaxen hair he had longed to knot in his hands. It was so soft and pliable, he was sure that Morgan's body would be the same if only . . . oh, God, if only . . .

Grant directed warm air on the hard-to-reach places, lifting the thick strands, parting the back, drawing sensuous circles with deliberate ease. When her hair was finally dry to the touch, he flicked the instrument off and proceeded with first the brush, then the comb. Morgan closed her eyes, relishing his languid manipulations. Finally his fingers continued with masterful exploits, massaging her temples and her nape.

His index fingers traced her jawline from her earlobes to her chin, lifting her face to him ever so gently. Since she was still sitting, he bent to meet her upraised, slightly parted lips with his luxurious kiss. She reveled in the taste of his mouth and marveled at the naturalness of it all.

Grant's hand trailed, quite naturally, down her arched neck, blazing paths of uncurbed passion through her veins. He tarried lazily over one firm, full breast. Morgan shuddered with desire as his thumb and forefinger rolled the already taut nipple playfully.

Weakly she fought her own dynamic response to Grant's fiery touch. "Grant, don't . . ."

He provokingly rubbed the tiny protrusion he held. "Don't deny what's happening between us, little one. You want me as badly as I want you," he murmured against her cheek. "Come to me. . . ."

As if drawn by an invisible force, Morgan reached up for him as he lifted her easily to her feet. Her hands pressed against his unyielding chest as she sought his lusty, powerful kiss. No more soft, gentle clinches, as with a low moan he crushed her to him vigorously, eliciting a sharp cry of agony from Morgan. Immediately the magic of the sensuous moment was broken, and Grant stepped back, muttering, "Damn! Did I hurt you, Morgan?"

She clutched her ribs and nodded, bending her head to hide the quick tears that sprang to her eyes.

"Morgan?"

She shook her head and the golden hair hid her face. "I'm . . . I'm sorry, Grant. I just can't—"

His voice was low and tense. "Morgan, I'll be careful. I swear it. God, I don't want to hurt you. But I want you."

"Grant, don't make unreasonable demands of me. I told you—"

Tightly he rasped, "Is it unreasonable for a man to want his wife?"

109

"Will you wrap this Ace bandage around me?" she demanded, holding up the beige item.

Grant looked at the bandage in her hand as if it were a foreign object that he had never before seen. *How could she make such a request? Didn't she realize what she was doing to him?* "Don't ask me to do that, Morgan," he said brusquely.

"Why not? I . . . need you, Grant. I can't do it myself. And the bandage helps ease the pain." She held the Ace bandage out to him.

He looked at it wildly, then back to her puzzled, chestnut eyes. "Nothing will ease the pain between us, Morgan, until you stop being so goddamn stubborn. Don't ask me to help you undress or to touch you again . . . until you're ready for me to stay!" Grant stalked out of the bedroom, leaving Morgan to hold the bandage alone and wonder why she had let him go.

He was right! She wanted him badly. And he had admitted that he wanted her. Why did she hold back? Why didn't she admit it? Was she scared of him? Of what would happen between them? Was she fearful of the pain? No—she quickly shoved that thought to the back of her mind. He had promised to be careful . . . that he didn't want to hurt her. Was she just too stubborn to give in to her husband? *To give in?* Why, she wanted him as much as he clamored after her.

Oh, Grant, I love you. Please come back to me to stay the night! She was astounded by her own thoughts—her own reluctant admission! *She loved Grant!* Was that it? Could it possibly be that she had fallen in love with this man she had chosen to be her husband? Her summer spouse? How did this happen? When? Her mind raced over their short, turbulent acquaintance . . . that fateful day in the hospital, his compliance on their wedding day, his arrogance the night he entered her room and announced he wouldn't live in the bunkhouse any longer. An irresistible smile formed as she recalled past scorching words, heated caresses, the feverish passion that engulfed them only moments ago. With a ragged sigh Morgan conceded that she loved Grant, and she wanted him to love her, too. Maybe that was why she hesitated. She wanted his love, not just his passion.

She could hear Grant's footsteps pacing the bare floor in the room next to hers, brief clanking of the typewriter, the crackling

110

of paper being ripped apart. His voice rumbled through the stillness of the night with muttered oaths. The old floor creaked with more pacing. He was as miserable as she. Finally when she could bear the sounds and her own torture no longer, Morgan walked steadily to his room. She knocked softly on the door. Maybe they could talk. . . .

Grant swung open the door, standing in the shadows dressed only in his briefs, looking so wild . . . so angry . . . so very masculine. She wanted him close to her—but she knew there would be no turning back this time. He had made that perfectly clear. And she knew it was too late for talking. They were beyond that now. With a shaky voice she appealed to her husband. "Grant, please come and hold me. I can't sleep."

He looked at her, unflinching and bold. "No, Morgan, I won't come and hold you anymore. I . . . just can't. But I will come and love you."

She nodded knowingly and looked down, not believing what she was doing. She only knew that she wanted him, too. At that moment—since the first time she had met him—for many long, miserable nights she had wanted him. "Okay."

"What did you say, Morgan?" he asked gruffly.

"Yes." She looked up at him, her bronze eyes meeting his passionate gaze. "I said yes!"

His voice was low and urgent. "Then say it, Morgan. Say you want me to love you."

His labored breathing was audible in the pause before she finally yielded, her voice a tremulous whisper. "Come and love me, Grant. I want you to love me."

Without a word he cradled her somber face in his hands and kissed her waiting lips, her pink-flushed cheeks, her closed eyelids. "Come on, little one. I'll bandage your ribs first. I . . . don't want to hurt you."

He led her into her bedroom, untied the shimmery robe and let it fall into a limp circle around her feet. With a sharp intake of tortuous air Grant's dove-gray eyes meandered down the gleaming whiteness of her breasts, her softly curved hips, her inviting thighs. Morgan stood brazenly exposed to Grant's blazing gaze, then passed the flesh-colored bandage to his hot, slightly trembling hands.

111

"Do you know how to do this?"

His voice was somewhat unsteady. "What? Oh . . . yes, I think I remember how the doctor wrapped it." He bent toward her and began to wind the bandage clumsily around her ribs while Morgan held her breasts up and out of his way. She hid the rosy tips from his close scrutiny and, shutting her eyes, pretended that he wasn't devouring her body with his eyes. And she tingled with anticipation.

"Is this too tight?" His fingers brushed her skin.

She shook her head and felt her hair ruffled around her shoulders, generating a shivering wave of desire down to the tips of her toes. He felt the tide, too. She was sure of it.

Slowly he spoke. "Morgan, you're beautiful. I've wanted to hold you, to touch you long before our wedding." His fingers swiftly clasped the bandage's end and pushed her hands away from the creamy mounds they hid. He then cupped them gently, moving his hands over them with sure gentle pressure. "Do you know how I've ached for you, little one? Do you know how hard this has been to work and live with you . . . and never touch you?" His skilled fingers rubbed lightly on the soft tips while he talked. "I hoped—prayed—that you would come to me. I knew you wanted me, too. Oh, God, the waiting has been torture!" By the time he stopped to take a breath, her nipples were prominent affirmations of Morgan's own aching responses to Grant's touch.

Her voice was a tight whisper. "How did you know? I didn't say anything to give you that impression."

His lips were close to hers, and his hands continued to caress her breasts maddeningly as he spoke. "You didn't have to say a thing. I could feel it. I saw beneath that angry exterior. I figured it was worth busting a couple of broncs to have you."

She shook her head. "I'm not worth risking your life over, Grant. I've felt guilty for setting you up to ride those broncs. I was so worried about . . . my husband."

His hands moved slowly downward to trace the shadowy outlines of her form, her waist, her hips, her thighs. "Suddenly, that word sounds right. Tonight I will be your husband, Morgan." He lifted her and carried her to the bed, lowering her tenderly on her back and kneeling beside her. He moved to touch the silky curve of her inner thighs, then to stroke her intimately.

112

His tongue began a sensuous journey along her thigh, trailing a path of kisses across her abdomen, then moving up to settle gently on a pink-tipped breast. Morgan quivered with unclaimed desire as his hands continued to explore her sensitive body.

"And I will be your wife—" She gasped softly as his lips brushed hers then sought again those delicious peaks, his tongue flicking in a sensual rhythm that threatened to drown her. She reached out to steady herself. "Grant . . . oh, Grant—"

"Do you want me?"

"You know . . . I do . . ."

"Then touch me. Let me know—" he rasped.

Tentatively, almost modestly, Morgan reached out for him. Her slender fingers raked curiously over Grant's chest and the small, erect male nipples. Her nails combed outrageously through the crisp mat of hair and followed its trail down his flat belly to the elastic waistband of his briefs. It was an easy effort to push them over his slim hips, but her hands halted abruptly when they transgressed to his rock-hard thighs. She was astounded at her boldness. Never before—

"Go ahead, Morgan—don't stop—" he grated hoarsely.

Carefully she averted her gaze and sought his deep gray eyes. "Grant, please . . . I—"

He stood and stepped out of the discarded briefs then sat down beside her again, his large, brown hands encircling her ivory shoulders. "I know, Morgan. I can hardly wait for you, too." He lay next to her and fervently pulled her on her side, into his welcoming arms. As the lengths of their bodies molded together, she realized the confirmation of his unyielding desire for her. "I crave you. But this moment is too beautiful to be rushed. I want to enjoy you slowly. And I want you to enjoy me, too." His mouth covered hers hungrily, his tongue teased her lips open until she welcomed him, touching the tip of his tongue with hers. A low moan escaped from his chest as he allowed her to tease, tempt, and plunder his mouth with her reckless, flicking tongue.

His hands caressed her back and stretched over her curved hips to pull her ardently to his own volatile warmth. He molded her silky softness to his firm, lengthy frame, thrusting his hips toward her instinctively.

Morgan buried her face in the curling hairs on his chest and

113

inhaled the close male scent of his skin. It was a sensuous, heady fragrance that increased her already-excited desires beyond believability. She ran her hand possessively down his side, delighting in the feel of the warm slope of his back, claiming every rib, every muscle, as her own. Moving her trembling palm in massaging strokes, she caressed the narrowness of his waist, the flare of his hips, and kneaded the muscled tautness of his thighs before exploring the tensed contours of his buttocks. She was astonished at her own willingness to make him a part of her.

From the depths of her feminine instinct, she was acutely aware that Grant's passion was rising to the summit of his endurance. She could feel his hard-muscled thighs, his firm chest, his masculine physique pressed excitingly against her. His lips found hers, his tongue outlining the softness of her mouth, as she breathlessly parted her lips to receive him. She tasted his sweet warmth and stretched out her arms to pull him even closer to her soft curves, but moaned aloud in pain.

"What is it?" he asked anxiously. "Did I—"

"No," she whispered with a sigh. "It was me. I forgot I have broken ribs. Can you believe I forgot so soon? I just wanted to pull you closer to me." She laughed lightly and rested her forehead against his solid chest, breathing deeply of his fragrance until the sharp pangs of pain subsided.

"Little one . . . little one . . ." He cradled her easily against his chest. "Come, let me make you my wife . . . officially . . . consummate our marriage. Mrs. LeMaster, tonight you are mine. And I am yours. We won't hurt those ribs, I promise." He gently pulled her on top of him, her breasts pressed into his chest. She felt him moving ever so slightly, easing her carefully until their bodies blended together. She smiled faintly, grateful for his gentleness.

He tilted her head up and looked deeply into her eyes, stroking the back of her neck, sending quiet ripples of desire down her spine. "Morgan, should I protect you? We never discussed it, since we hadn't planned on this."

Her voice was subdued. "I'm taking the pill, Grant, for medical reasons, and have been for a long time . . . Grant, could I make a small request? Please . . . turn out the light."

114

"Why? You have a beautiful body, and I want to see you when I love you, little one."

Morgan's bronze eyes traveled over his face, reaching his eyes in a pleading gaze. "Please, Grant . . . make it dark."

With an exasperated sigh he turned and switched the small lamp. "There! Is that better? Nothing in sight."

Morgan's voice sounded small in the darkness of the room. "Yes, Grant, much better . . ." How could she tell him that her lack of experience precluded any preference?

The bed dipped slightly when Grant shifted beneath her. He lay quietly for a moment, and she could feel the heat radiating from his body. Oh, God, what was she doing? Suddenly old fears welled up inside her to replace the confidence and desires she had felt with Grant only moments ago. His hand stroked her back and she gasped audibly at his touch. *Should she tell him?*

His fingers made sensuous circles on her buttocks. "Easy, little one. Just relax, honey. I told you, I won't hurt your ribs."

"Grant, I . . ." *She had to explain her reluctance.* "Can your wife make a confession?"

"Of course, darling," he murmured, his lips excitingly caressing the curve of her neck, as his tongue drew glistening patterns on her silky skin.

"I'm not very . . . experienced. There's been only one other man in my life." *There. That should be enough.*

His voice was muffled as he nestled his face at the base of her throat. "Only one? In your life . . . or in your bed?"

"Grant, this is serious." She giggled nervously. "In my bed!"

"Honey, I must admit, I didn't think you were entirely innocent. But I'm still jealous! I want you all to myself!"

Morgan twirled her fingers in the hair on his chest, and raised herself slightly, then lowered her head to caress a hardened nipple with her lips. "Don't be jealous. This is where I want to be . . . with you, Grant."

"Where? In Europe? Was it . . . were you in love?" His raspy breathing halted, but she could feel the heated pounding of his heart.

Her hand moved up his strained neck, along the squared jawline to outline his lips with her eager fingers. "Yes, in

Europe," she managed, then paused to take in a tremulous breath. "It was . . . awful."

"Damn!" Grant hissed, his hot breath steaming her cheek. "Damn, I hate him! That's why you've held back from me. Even tonight. You're scared. Morgan honey, I'm sorry . . . I hope I can make you want to love again." There was a gentleness in his tone.

Morgan's fingers silenced his lips. "Grant, I . . . I held back for . . . love. And I'm not scared of you. Please love me tonight. Teach me to be your wife."

"Yes, little one, I'll love you . . . gently and completely." And he nuzzled her earlobe, kissing a fiery path to the throbbing hollow of her throat. His purpose was different now. He wanted to give, not just receive.

Grant carefully eased her onto her back and stretched alongside her, propping himself up on one elbow.

His finger slowly traced the outline of her trembling body, stopping finally at the soft cushion of her breast where it lightly awakened her nipple into prominence. He knelt beside her, bending forward to continue his teasing game with his tongue, going from one satiny slope to the other, lovingly flicking her nipples.

His hands caressed her abdomen, causing a fluttering to begin deep within her. With one hand he gradually provoked the warmth of her femininity, carrying her to a height of passion that threatened to consume her. She strained toward his touch as it liberated her to joys she had never before experienced. Finally she cried out to him . . . softly . . . but it was a plea nevertheless. Grant responded by carefully moving her over him, acclaiming the triumphant glory between a man and his wife. He had long awaited her touch, her response, and now, as she pressed her body into his, he knew the ecstasy was shared by both of them. Oh, how he had longed to take her, to claim her body. She was his wife, and now he would truly know her as he should.

The waiting was over, and as he lifted her to meet his urgent need, he exalted that there was no stopping now. Forgotten were the hateful words, the unfair reasons for their marriage, the unfulfilled past. Nothing mattered in those frenzied, mindless seconds when the lovers reached the once-distant peaks of satisfaction . . . together. *Together, at last!* A sharp cry escaped

Morgan's lips. A cry of love . . . a cry of pain. But there was no stopping, for either of them. Finally Grant, in the moment of complete release, clutched her shuddering body to him and they slumped exhaustedly against each other, riding out their sharing of the exquisite passion that slowly eased out of their bodies.

Morgan sighed, totally at peace, as she sensuously slid down the length of his body and curled on the mattress beside him.

Grant shifted to look at her face. "Are you all right? I didn't mean to hurt you."

She gazed lovingly into his passion-darkened eyes. *Did she see love there?* "I'm fine."

He kissed her nose affectionately, then her lips. "I always knew it would be like that with us, Morgan . . . perfect."

Shyly she answered, "I know I wasn't much of a lover, Grant, between my damned cracked ribs and lack of experience." Suddenly she was filled with a rush of emotion, and unavoidable tears swam in her large, bronze eyes. Was it body-wracking passion or the joy of love . . . fulfilled at last? She squeezed her eyes shut.

"Morgan, look at me." Grant's voice was still thick with emotion. Framing her face with his large hands, his thumbs wiped away the tears. "Was it that bad, little one? I want you to enjoy our love as much as I do."

She pulled his hand to her mouth and kissed the palm. "It was wonderful, Grant. These are tears of joy. It's just that . . . I . . . wanted love . . . not lust. I want your love, Grant."

"You have my love, Morgan," he murmured huskily against her cheek, moving his lips to hers. "You're a wonderful lover, little one. Next time will be better, I promise."

"Next time? Promise?" She smiled through her tears.

"Oh, yes, Morgan. This is just the beginning for us. We have a lifetime of love ahead. You'll enjoy it more . . . I'll see to that."

"I couldn't enjoy you more, Grant." *A lifetime together? Not just one short summer?* Her heart skipped at the thought. She could feel them both relaxing, and it filled her with a deep feeling of contentment.

"The first time is never the best, honey. Each time we love will be better than the last. I promise. But in order to improve we have to practice."

"Practice, huh?" She giggled. "Don't forget you have an injured wife who knows as much about making love as she does about breaking wild horses!"

"Forget the horses. I'll teach you the rest."

And he did. Grant's kiss was as gentle as his love for her, and Morgan eagerly responded to his promises and passions throughout the night.

CHAPTER EIGHT

Grant glanced up from his early-morning coffee. "Well, good morning, little one! What are you doing up so early?" He sat alone at the table while Willa busily prepared her usual breakfast feast in the kitchen.

Morgan smiled happily at her husband, placing one affectionate arm on his shoulder. "I'm missing too much by staying in bed all day. And that's no fun."

He rose and kissed her sweet, smiling lips thoroughly. "I figured after last night you'd need a few more days of recuperation," he murmured just loud enough for her to hear.

Morgan blushed, but responded smartly, "After last night I should be capable of anything, short of horseback riding!"

Grant grinned devilishly at her. "Well said!" Then he glanced at the polite sounds nearby. "Look who's up, Willa!"

The older woman smiled broadly. "Morgan, honey! Good morning! How are you feeling? Don't you think it's too soon for you to be getting up? And so early in the day!" Willa was obviously concerned about the welfare of her self-appointed charge and continued to hover like a clucking hen, even though her charge was determined not to be hovered over any longer. At least not by Willa.

"I'm much better, thank you, Willa, thanks to excellent nursing care from you and Grant. And you're right about it being awfully early. I think a cup of coffee would help to wake me up."

"Oh, sure!" Willa hurried for the coffee while Grant helped Morgan sit comfortably.

"Morgan, I think Willa's right. It's too soon for you to be up and about," Grant commented seriously.

"You didn't think so last night," she countered.

He leaned close and jibed, "I'm for keeping you in bed all the time, myself!"

David's happy voice interrupted the loving look and mutual desires smoldering between them. "Hi, Morgan! Are you going to have breakfast with us? Are you well now?"

She smiled a happy greeting to the youngster. "Hi, David! I'm not completely well, but I'm much better. And I'm tired of lying around in bed all day. I miss all the fun!"

Grant's eyes caught hers with a teasing glimmer as David joined them at the table and continued talking. "Can we go fishing today, Grant? And can we have another picnic? Huh?"

Morgan sipped her steamy coffee. "I doubt it, David. There's too much work to be done. I'm anxious to get back to work."

Grant refilled his own coffee cup and pondered aloud, "As a matter of fact, there isn't much happening today. You'll be happy to know that we've sold Blue Velvet. They're coming after him tomorrow. Next week Boyd and I are picking up several horses from a ranch south of Bayfield. So today will be rather slow."

"Then we can go! Oh, boy!" David's face was exuberant.

"Now hold on, pardner," Grant hedged, trying to calm his son. "I don't think Morgan's up to tromping across the fields and climbing on rocks to fish."

As Willa set heaping plates of eggs and biscuits for everyone, she suggested, "Morgan definitely needs to take it easy, but I'll bet she's up to a ride over to Mesa Verde. I could pack you three a picnic lunch and you could spend the day."

Grant greeted the idea enthusiastically. "Willa, that's a great idea! How does it sound to you, Morgan? Would you like a little ride to the Indian ruins? I think David will find it very interesting."

Morgan nodded in agreement. "I haven't been there in years, and I'd love it. I'm sure David would, too."

"Indian ruins? What's that? Can you fish there?" David asked curiously.

Grant shook his head. "No. No fishing. But there's lots to see."

"No fishing?" David puckered his small face. "Then why would I like it?"

Grant reached over and tousled his son's dark hair. "Just wait and see. Trust me, David. You'll like it."

It was a couple of hours before they were ready to set out for their excursion. Grant and Boyd quickly finished up morning chores, Willa prepared the picnic lunch she promised, and Morgan dressed very slowly, with a little help from her husband. The project was delayed considerably as Grant admired and savored the newly discovered, warm curves of his wife. He spent substantially more time dressing her than he had undressing. And of course, in a conscious effort to avoid hurting her injured ribs, Grant took the time to be abundantly careful. And impassionately romantic.

Finally a small, impatient voice outside the bedroom door rushed their efforts. "Morgan! Aren't you ready *yet*?"

"Almost ready, David!" called Morgan, giggling against her husband's chest. "Come on, Grant. David's waiting."

"Kids!" groaned Grant, good-naturedly. "Oh, all right. This day is for him. But don't forget, the nights are reserved for us, Morgan." He tweaked her nose and began to pull on his jeans.

As the three left the ranch house, Grant pulled Boyd aside. "You and Willa take the day off, Boyd. You both deserve it. Take your wife out to eat and to a movie this evening." He winked and clapped his friend on the back before joining his small family in the car.

The trip to Mesa Verde took about two hours. In that brief time they traveled from the lush woodland of the San Juan Mountain area to the semiarid land of mesas and canyons. Morgan was always amazed at the transformation of the landscape between Durango and the green table, as the Indians called it. Aspens and ponderosa gave way to piñon and scrub oak and juniper and cactus. It was a strange, yet beautiful, transformation.

As the winding road hairpinned to the flat top of the huge

121

mesa, there was a growing anticipation to witness the centuries-old villages hidden deep in the canyons. There, tucked into widemouthed sandstone arches in the sides of the cliffs, lay proof of the lives of ancient people in this rather hostile land. It was a secret concealed from modern civilization until this century.

Morgan glanced across the front seat at the dark-haired contour of her husband. He seemed lost in thought today as he quietly guided them to the place that time forgot. She wondered what secrets of his past were hidden by time, and if she would ever know all about him. She already knew he was a different man from the one she thought she had married. He was definitely his own man and would not be dominated by her. Mysterious, yet magnetic, tough and obstinate, Grant was also very sensitive and passionate. Who was this man she had married? Morgan would probably ask herself that question a hundred times before she knew the answer.

Actually they had just begun to know each other last night. *Last night!* She tingled inside and felt her cheeks tinge at the remembrance. The passions Grant had awakened in her were beyond her wildest yearning . . . even her most wanton imagination. She had never believed it possible for her to desire a man as she did Grant. And, even as he had predicted, she had brazenly gone to him! She had actually asked him to make love to her! And oh, God—*did he!*

But was it love? Was it really Grant's love that influenced his intense and skillful lovemaking? Or was it his passion gone wild? How could she be sure?

Morgan had always dreamed that the man she loved would elicit her passion and her love, the feelings she now had for Grant . . . had felt last night. And yet she wasn't even sure of her own love. It was all too new. She glanced again at him, remembering his words spoken in the quiet satisfaction of her embrace. *You have my love, Morgan.* Did he really mean it? Or did he intimate that they were lovers driven together by their own desires?

Maybe it was her own desires thrusting her into this man's arms—this man who was her husband. It had happened before. Only . . . with André, there had been no fulfillment. And the intensity of their relationship was nothing like what was happen-

ing between her and Grant. It had ended long ago in Greece.
. . .

"Would you like to walk down to Long House with us, Morgan? This is the largest of the cliff dwellings here, and it's like taking a walk back in time."

The warm sound of Grant's voice jarred Morgan back to the present, and as she gazed at him with love in her eyes, she knew she didn't want to leave the present time and place. She wanted to be here, in love with Grant, and receiving his love. She smiled and nodded, enticing him with her glow of love. Unable to resist, he kissed her lips instinctively.

His voice was a bare whisper. "Save that look for me tonight. Right now we'd better hurry to catch up with David."

Hand-in-hand, they followed him into the ancient silent city that was nestled in the arched cave of the huge sandstone cliff. After listening to the guide's exposition, the three milled around the ruins on their own. It was easy to imagine ghosts of the past going about their daily lives. Morgan sat on a shaded wall as Grant tried to explain the significance of the Indian ruins to David in terms the boy could understand.

"People lived in these little stone houses seven hundred years ago, David!"

David looked around with renewed interest. "Did kids live here, too? Kids like me?"

Grant nodded. "Sure, David. Entire families lived here with their kids. Doesn't that sound like fun?"

"You mean whole families like us and Morgan? Yeah, that would be fun! Would you like that, Morgan? If our family lived here instead of the ranch?" David's large, dark eyes were positive reminders of his ancestors.

She smiled at his exuberance. "Yes, it would be fun, David. Climbing up the steep rocks using those little footholes might give me some problems, though!"

He looked straight up at the small indentions in the rocky cliffs. "They might be hard for me, too. I think I'd miss the ranch . . . and the ice cream!"

Morgan tousled his straight, raven hair and laughed. "That's right, David! There was no ice cream in those days! We'd both miss that!"

He propped small fists on his hips and assessed the situation in his own, youthful insight. "I think I like our family just the way it is right now. Don't you, Grant?"

The man looked gently at his young son, then seriously at Morgan. "Yes, David. I like things just the way they are right now. Couldn't be better, huh, Morgan?" His hand slipped around her hips affectionately, while the other hand encircled his son's shoulders.

"Yes, the Anasazi missed a lot living here in these rocky cliffs." Grant heaved himself up to sit beside Morgan on the wall, their legs touching intimately.

David climbed up beyond where they sat and curiously peeked into a small, square window. His voice was filled with wonder. "Where did these Anasazi people put the TV?"

Both Grant and Morgan laughed at the child's twentieth-century view of routine life. "They didn't have TV in those days, son. They didn't even have electricity," Grant explained.

"Wasn't it awfully dark up here at night?" David's ebony eyes scanned the ancient block buildings that towered above them.

"I'm sure it was," Grant conceded. "But they had campfires that provided light and heat as well as a place to cook. There are still traces of campfires. Do you see the groove in this big rock? The Anasazi women used another round, smooth rock, like this, to grind their corn by hand. It made a cornmeal for their bread. These rocks are called *mano y metate.*"

Morgan eyed the demonstration skeptically, grateful that she didn't have to hunker over the *mano y metate* to grind their food today. However David was far more interested in what the ancients ate than the process of preparing the food. "What kind of bread? Was that all they ate?"

Grant shrugged. " I suppose it was flat bread, like a tortilla. But they also grew corn and squash along the top of the mesa." He pointed at the brush-covered land above the sandstone arches and cliff dwellings. "They ate corn on the cob."

David nodded, for obviously some of what Grant was explaining was familiar. Most Indian children knew tales of their ancient ancestors, and David was no exception. "My grandmother grew corn and squash, too. We had a campfire sometimes and she let me roast marshmallows." The small, brown boy walked around the peculiar circular wall where Grant and Morgan sat. When he reached them, he hunkered down solemnly. "She also told me stories about the Anasazi. She said that in the round *kiva* strange things happened. Sometimes good, sometimes bad. Do you believe that?"

Grant tried to dispel unfounded fears in the mind of his small son. "No one is really sure, of course, but they think the *kiva* —this area here—was a ceremonial place. And I suppose things that are strange to us happened here. But look, David, we're sitting in a *kiva* right now, and it seems perfectly safe to me."

David picked up a tiny rock and tossed it. His smile reflected the relief he felt. "Me, too! Did my mother have ice cream and TV?"

"I'm sure she did." Grant's large hand rested securely on David's small shoulder.

An eerie silence settled over the abandoned Indian ruins, broken only by the plaintive call of a red-tailed hawk, which circled overhead. All of the visitors had gone, leaving Grant and Morgan and David sitting alone atop the ancient wheel-shaped wall.

"What about my father? Did he ever take her to get ice cream, the way you do Morgan and me?"

Morgan caught the gasp in her throat before it became audible.

"I don't know, David," Grant muttered gruffly, aware of the acute crisis that had suddenly been created.

"Where is he? Could we ask him?" David began to climb down off the wall.

"No, David. I don't think so." The silence around the words was deafening.

There was a shocking honesty in the small, brown face as David declared, almost casually, "Well, I don't care. He didn't love me and my grandmother, so I don't love him. Anyway, you're my new father, and I love you, Grant. And Morgan. I like this family best of all. I hope we're always like this."

He was too young to notice the dark concern in Grant's face, and the stricken astonishment in Morgan's. His statement was made, and, childlike, his attention rambled quickly to other things.

125

"Can I climb down to that big flat rock over there?" He pointed down the arroyo.

Grant nodded silently, avoiding Morgan's alarmed, questioning eyes until David was out of earshot.

Morgan's voice quivered slightly. "Grant? What was he talking about?"

Grant looked at her and sighed heavily. "Out of the mouths of babes . . . come remarkable truths. I think that was a beautiful compliment from David, Morgan. We've only been a part of his life a short while—"

Morgan's tone was alarm filled, and her statement flat. "He's not your child, is he, Grant?"

Grant pressed his lips together tightly. "Not yet. I'm in the process of adopting him."

Rage shook her being. "Adopting David? Then why didn't you tell me? I'm only your wife!"

"You weren't until last night!" he accused.

"Grant, please. I am your wife! We've shared—" Her voice quivered as she recalled the intimacy they had shared the night before.

But his voice was steel-edged. "Morgan, you've got to admit, until last night we'd shared nothing!"

She shook her head slowly, ignoring his inference. "Why . . . why couldn't you tell me such an important thing as this? Adopting David . . . adopting . . ." She mulled the words aloud as if trying to digest them. And indeed she was. The whole idea created a huge knot in her stomach.

"Morgan, try to understand me. It's because this issue is so important and sensitive that I held back until the timing was right. There are a lot of legal ramifications involved here. I needed certain credentials for this adoption."

Yet Morgan could not hide the hurt and resentment she felt as she snapped, "And now's the right time? It seems to me David picked the time and, in his innocence, revealed more than you wanted me to know!" Her voice echoed against the empty stones around them.

Grant's voice was lower, gentler. "This isn't exactly how I planned to tell you. But I did want you to know—of course I did! And now I'm . . . I'm glad it's out in the open."

126

"It doesn't matter now, does it? At least, it's after we've been to bed together! After the bonds of our marriage have been sealed! After you've—"

"No!" he interrupted. His large hands reached out to her, trying to grasp her shoulders. "My God, Morgan! Our relationship has nothing to do with David!"

Morgan twisted away from his touch. "The hell it doesn't! All the time I thought . . . I thought we were . . . like a little family. Just as David said—" She choked on the knot that had now settled in her throat, causing tears to fill her sorrel eyes. But she continued. "I thought things were beginning to work out for us. We—you and me—were just starting. And David seems so happy, and it's like we really belong together."

"We do belong together, Morgan. It's all still the same."

"No! It's not the same! You lied to me! You lied by not telling me all about David! How do you expect us to build a relationship without truth?"

Grant's lips stiffened angrily. "I did not lie!"

Defiantly she answered, "It's all the same! You were unfair to let me believe what was wrong!"

"Unfair? You have the nerve to accuse me of being unfair? You—who asked me to alter my life long enough to marry you so you could get your own life straightened out? You have a warped sense of fairness, Morgan!" He moved to his feet like the lithe Indians that stalked this land so many years ago.

"Is that how you think of me, Grant? Of our . . . marriage? That it's unfair—that I've inconvenienced your life?" Hot tears trailed her cheeks as she fought for control of her wildly raging emotions.

Grant's gray eyes narrowed as he commented cruelly, "You'd better think again before you call what we have a marriage!"

Morgan pulled herself to her feet. "Well, I think you just saw the opportunity to grab some quick bucks and a chance to crawl into my bed as well!" With a deep sense of abhorrence she regretted her capitulation last night. Oh, how could she have been so stupid . . . again?

"Frankly, Morgan, you can think what you damn well please because I don't care! And my business with David is none of your concern!" His heartless words ripped through her, leaving Mor-

127

gan feeling as vacant and empty as the Indian ruins surrounding her.

As she watched Grant's back disappear, she muttered angrily, "Damn you, Grant LeMaster! I hate you!" But her words were snatched up by the wind and flung against the sandstone arches and never reached him.

Strong gusts swept through the deep arroyo and whined around Morgan's lone figure, drying her bitter tears and whipping her long blond hair around her head in an unruly aura. She began to walk, aimlessly following the circle of the *kiva*. Overpowered by the crush of intense silence, the impact of her conversation with Grant left her chilled and bereft. It had all happened so fast . . . one minute they were a happy little family, the next there was an abysmal chasm between them. One moment Grant was declaring that they belonged together, the next he was asserting that this business with David was none of her concern! How could he possibly expect her to simply excise all interest and affection for David? After all, she cared deeply for him—had grown to love him, as she did Grant.

No, what she felt for Grant couldn't be love. He made her feel too awful . . . like now. The things he said and did were too cruel, too harsh for love. What had happened between her and Grant could be summed up in one word—sex. Shamefully Morgan admitted it to herself. They had each responded to the passion of the moment without regard to sensitivity. What they'd shared was an emotionless reaction to physical closeness. *Or was it?* They had exchanged words of love . . . words *about* love. There was a difference.

Suddenly Morgan was overwhelmed with an eerie sensation. The ghosts of the vanquished seemed to hover all around her, crying with the wind, screaming at the fair-haired intruder. She was encroaching on their sacred land just as she was invading the lives of Grant and David. And she didn't belong.

She looked around, half expecting to see a bronze, leather-clad body lurking in the crumbling ruins. But she was alone. Maybe David's Indian grandmother was right, that strange things did happen in the *kiva*. After all, it was here in the ancient ceremonial place that the truth had been revealed. Truth Grant had tried to hide from her. What else was he hiding? Oh, dear God—who was this man she had married? And what other secrets was he hiding?

Impetuously another thought struck her. Maybe Grant was David's real father, after all! Maybe he was the man who had fathered the Indian child, then abandoned him! And now she was caught in the midst of Grant's personal guilt and legal battle to compensate for the sins of his past! Damn him, anyway! No, she couldn't love him. All she wanted to do was to get away from Grant . . . and the exotic, prehistoric, Indian cliff dwellings. Both were formidable.

Slowly Morgan climbed the carved-out stone steps alone, returning with dread to face Grant and David, who waited by the car.

Grant generously handed her the remainder of his Coke and offered, "Here, finish this. I know you're thirsty."

She accepted the drink silently and gulped thirstily. *Do you also know how much I'm hurting inside?*

"Let's have lunch, Morgan. I'm hungry," David suggested.

"Good idea, David!" Grant agreed before Morgan could respond. "Why don't we find a nice place for a picnic. Maybe we can hike down into an arroyo. There are other cliff dwellings around here, you know."

They found a place to park the car and hiked in seclusion to Mug House, another of the cliff dwellings. Their picnic was quiet and tense with David doing most of the talking. Afterward David and Grant explored the rugged, rocky-cliffed terrain while Morgan waited in the shade of a huge boulder. It gave her some much-needed time alone to mull over today's revelations.

Finally they returned, David leading the way. "Morgan! Are you ready to go home?"

"Sure." She smiled lovingly at the weary little boy. No matter whose child he was, he had worked his way to her heart. She began gathering the picnic supplies.

As Grant approached, he added, "David's had it for today. He's exhausted!"

Morgan glanced caustically at the tall, perspiration-drenched man who followed the still-active child. "Looks to me like David's not the only one who's exhausted. I dare say he's done better today than you!"

129

Grant doffed his straw cowboy hat and wiped his dripping brow. "Undoubtedly!" he admitted with a devilish grin. "Of course, my energy was expended before the day began!"

Morgan's spicy brown eyes condemned him as she asserted, "Well, we'll see that you get plenty of rest from now on!"

David took her hand, pulling her impatiently along the path. "I wish you could have come with us, Morgan. We saw some broken pots that the Anasazi used. And I looked for arrowheads!"

"Sounds like fun, David."

"Uh-huh. But this isn't funner than fishing, is it, Morgan?"

Morgan smiled at the tired but truthful child, then cast a glance at Grant. "Well, David, this has been . . . enlightening, but not as much fun as fishing. I see at least one of us is being completely honest today."

"Can we stop in Durango for ice cream, Grant? Can we, huh?" Anticipation lit David's ebony eyes.

"Sure, David," Grant acquiesced. "Maybe it'll salvage the day."

"Yeah! Ice cream!" David ran ahead up the path.

"Nothing can salvage what's been said today," Morgan claimed icily.

Grant grabbed her arm and made her turn to hear him. "How about the truth?"

"I think I've heard enough confessions for today!"

His hand tightened on her wrist. "You haven't heard nearly enough, Morgan!"

"You're hurting my arm!" Morgan hissed under her breath. "Let go, damn you! I don't intend to listen to any more of your half-truths! Anyway, David's waiting."

The long trip home was silent and strained. Both Morgan and David had reached their maximum endurance and settled comfortably in the roomy Suburban. David curled in the backseat and was asleep in no time. As the sun dropped from view in a glorious, red-orange blaze beyond Mesa Verde Indian Ruins, Morgan dozed. Through the treacherous, hairpin curves, the flat farmland, the rise of mountains around Durango, Morgan slept soundly against the shoulder of the man she wanted to hate.

The journey home was interrupted by the brief, promised

stopover in Durango for ice cream. When the Suburban finally jolted to a stop in front of the Rocking M, Morgan roused and pushed herself away from Grant.

"Are we home yet?" David asked sleepily from the backseat.

"Okay, you two sleepyheads, wake up! We're home!" Grant announced as he turned to help David out and unload the picnic supplies.

Home? Morgan wondered vaguely as she stumbled inside the dark ranch house. *How can Grant call this home? He's here under duress. But then, so am I.* With a wearisome sigh she entered her bedroom alone. She heard the muffled sounds as Grant packed David into bed and pondered sadly how long they would occupy this house and her life. She felt now that it had been a big mistake to involve them. At one time it had seemed so simple. Grant could help her achieve her goal, she would pay him handsomely, and he would leave with no regrets. *No regrets!* She hadn't counted on her own emotional involvement and concern for this man she now called her husband. And his son . . . she shuddered at the thought and the deception.

Morgan stepped into the shower, attempting to wash away the futility of her relationship with Grant and the exhaustion of her body. However she accomplished neither. Her muscles still ached for rest, and her soul longed for reprieve from Grant's possession. Sleep, she reasoned, would satisfy both desires. She pulled her robe over her nakedness and turned down the covers of her bed just as Grant entered the bedroom.

Morgan faced him wearily, exhaustion obvious in her face, but spirit in her voice. "Get out of my bedroom! I've had enough of your lies today!" She wondered where she got her bravado, for inside she trembled. He seemed to tower ominously over her and had proven he could overpower her. Now, with her rib injury, she was completely helpless. *What was she thinking? He was her husband! He wouldn't—*

"Oh, no!" Grant laughed wickedly and leaned arrogantly against the dresser. There was a heartless quality to his voice that was both alarming and infuriating. "I've come to see if I can help *my wife* out of her clothes! Do you need a man tonight? Or maybe you need me to bandage your ribs! I'm good at wrapping ribs!

131

Or maybe you just need a wrangler who'll bust his ass on your goddamn ranch for room and board!"

Morgan raised her chin defiantly. "You got more than room and board last night! Now what do you want? I told you to get out of here! If you think this night will be as rewarding as last, it'll have to be by force! You'll have to rape your wife, Grant LeMaster!"

His lips curled contemptibly. "Don't flatter yourself, Morgan! I'll never take you by force. I came to talk. Then you can go to bed *alone*."

Her brown eyes flashed. "We have nothing to say."

He folded his long, powerful arms across his solid chest. "Yes, we do. I have some things to straighten out with my wife . . . David's adoptive mother."

"Don't . . . don't call me . . . that." She nearly choked on the words.

"Why not, Morgan? Does being an instant mother scare you? Well, don't worry. It won't be for long. In fact I came very close to just taking him with me and leaving this place tonight. I feel an urgency to go somewhere that no one can find us . . . so they can't take him away from me." Grant's voice ended with a sober, hard-edged tone. When Morgan didn't answer, he continued. "But I know that won't help David. Most of all, it won't help the adoption. It would only serve to confuse him even more. And, God knows, he's confused enough about his life already."

Angrily Morgan defended the child. "What do you expect? Even I am confused. If you'd start telling the truth—"

"David knows the truth! He knows his father was a white man who left before he was born. He knows his mother was a beautiful Navajo woman who died when he was born. And he knows that I'm trying to adopt him and . . ." Grant's voice became strained and somewhat hoarse. ". . . that I love him."

Morgan folded her arms boldly. "Does he know you're his real father? That you fathered him and left his mother alone when she was pregnant, then became plagued with guilt after all these years?" Morgan knew she was drawing heavily from her own speculation and, by the shadow on Grant's face, treading dangerous ground. But she wanted the truth this time from Grant and was willing to risk his wrath.

132

Grant's steel-cold eyes hardened at her accusation. He took a step closer and gripped her forearms angrily. Through clenched teeth he muttered, "David's not my child! Damn you, Morgan! Haven't you had enough of unfounded allegations from your family? Now you've done the same to me!"

His stinging reply smacked across her as if he had raised his hand physically against her. Suddenly Morgan felt sick and miserable at the truth of his accusation. She hadn't even given Grant a chance at the truth, just as they had never listened to her.

"Grant . . . I . . . I'm sorry. . . . I just . . ." she stammered, groping for the right words, which never came.

His face came within inches of hers, and once again his musky scent reached her. "I will tell you this, Morgan. David is not of my blood—but that doesn't matter a damn to me! He will be my *real* son very soon. And it will be accomplished with your help, too!" He released her then, and shoved her away as if repulsed by her closeness.

She touched her throbbing arms where he had gripped so tightly. "My help? Hardly!" What did he want from her now?

"Oh, yes! You'll sign the adoption request saying you're my new wife . . . and David's prospective mother. I upheld my end of the bargain. Now it's your turn!"

Bargain? Is that what he thought of their . . . relationship? Had she imagined it was more? Oh, what a fool she had been! "I don't see how you can ask anything of me. Why would I help you, anyway?"

Grant's answer was simple and hard-hitting. "Only for David's sake. I am all he has."

Morgan sighed raggedly. "Grant, why didn't you tell me the truth? All this time I thought he was your child. And now—"

Grant spread his hands with a shrug. "Why should I tell you? And risk that you wouldn't marry me and give me what I needed most for the adoption—a wife? You probably wouldn't have signed that marriage contract. But you were willing to sign anything in exchange for my name on your marriage license."

Morgan shook as she realized what she had done. "You're very devious, Grant LeMaster. You knew that if I didn't sign the contract, I would have as much legal claim to David as you . . . if we ever end this marriage."

"But we don't have to worry about that now, do we? I'll never let you have him. I'm the one who fought for him. I'm the one who'll keep him. Don't you understand? No, I . . . I guess you couldn't." He looked away and ran his hand through his dark hair.

"Try me."

Grant looked at her deeply, trying to analyze her sincerity. Then, he sat on the edge of her bed, heaved a sigh, and began to speak, as if in a daze. "I was in Ignacio at the Ute tribal office working on a story when they brought him in. Someone had found him eating out of . . . the city dump . . . and he looked like a wild boy. You wouldn't have recognized him. His hair was long and matted, and he was just skin and bones. All you could see were those big, brown eyes. The Sheriff's Department determined that David's grandmother had died two weeks earlier in the mountains where they lived. The clincher was that he isn't Ute. He's Navajo. So they had to return him to his tribal government down in Arizona. Since he had no family, and was obviously a half-breed, he would probably end up a ward of the state, white man's problem. I watched them toss around the options for this little kid all afternoon. Well, the chief and I had become friendly, and I managed to convince him that I would take good care of the boy. But one look into those eyes of David's, and I was hooked. Within the week I filed for adoption with the Indian Child Welfare Department of the Navajo Tribe. The hearing is set for next month."

"And I came along just in time to provide the stable family life you needed to prove yourself a fit father for that adoption," Morgan finished bitterly.

He shrugged his admittance. "Something like that."

"Damn you, Grant! Why didn't you just tell me? Why weren't you truthful right up front? We could have worked something out for David. Instead you used me! And managed to get into my bed, too!" Tears filled Morgan's sorrel eyes.

Grant rose and faced her menacingly. "How the hell can you stand there so self-righteously? You used me, too! You wanted a husband for your own personal gain and a strong back to run

134

this damned ranch! Well, you've got both! You're just angry because I turned the tables on you and took advantage of the marriage, too. You selfish bitch! It's all right for you, but not for me!"

Morgan blanched at his accusations. "No! That's not what I meant. I just want us to be truthful—"

"Truthful?" He laughed scornfully. "Okay, Morgan. Let's be truthful. As for last night in your bed—I was there because I wanted to be. And so were you. I didn't have to go through all this hell to get into a woman's bed. I wanted *you*. And don't forget you invited me there! There was no force and you damn well know it."

"Grant, please—"

"Let me finish, Morgan dear, and you can go to bed alone, as I promised. I'll assure you of one thing. I love that kid in there. And you'd better not try to do a thing to interfere with my keeping him or . . . you'll regret it. I'll do anything to keep him, Morgan, and don't you ever forget it!"

"Anything?"

"Anything!" And he stalked out, keeping his promise to stay away from her bed.

However, as tired as she was, Morgan found sleep elusive.

135

CHAPTER NINE

Despite her sleepless night Morgan stumbled to the breakfast table early. She had no desire to lie in bed for another sleepless hour. "Just coffee, please, Willa." She averted her red-rimmed eyes from Grant's sharp gaze and concentrated on the steam rising from her coffee cup.

He refused to ignore her and reached over to cover her shaky hand with his. "What are you doing up so early?" There was no softness in his voice, and Morgan was aware of the exchange of knowledgeable glances between Willa and Boyd.

Damn! Why did Grant have to be so obvious about their conflicts? There was a world of difference between his sweet, loving greeting of yesterday morning and now. Morgan was determined not to be intimidated by Grant or their personal clashes. She slipped her hand from his warm touch. "I've stayed in bed too long already. This dude ranch needs a lot of work."

"You're in no shape to do any work, Morgan, and you know it."

Her sable eyes flashed at him. "I'm fully aware of what I'm capable of doing . . . and what I'm not able to do." How dare he question her!

He sighed as if dealing with a recalcitrant child. "Well, if you insist on being up and around, why don't you work on the books? Nobody has had time to organize an accounting system for the Rocking M Ranch. There are already several bills that should be

136

paid and a brand-new ledger is on the desk. Do something useful today." With that he walked out, his heavy boot step punctuating his taciturn statements.

Morgan gripped her coffee cup, repressing the primitive urge to hurl it at Grant's receding back. Instead she clutched it tightly, gathering control of her raging emotions. This lack of control seemed rampant whenever she clashed with Grant, which was quite frequent. But then he was so demanding and harsh, living with him was nearly impossible. That almost ended last night, yet Grant went about his work this morning as if nothing had happened between them. Oh, but it had. In the last two days they had drawn together into intimacy, then hurled apart with vicious accusations. She couldn't dissolve the question in her mind of how they would manage through the summer. Then David joined her at the table, and she wondered with inner pain what would happen to them all by the end of the summer.

After forcing some breakfast with David, Morgan ambled into the small room they had turned into the office. She surveyed the disarray of papers scattered about and the neat, never-opened ledger and realized with a jab of anger that Grant was right. Someone needed to work on the books. And it might as well be her.

Morgan spent most of the next two days at the desk, organizing, figuring, writing, filing, working herself into exhaustion so that she could fall asleep nights. It was the only way she could get any rest.

"We'll be working in the red until late July or early August at this rate, Morgan," Grant assessed, pouring over her neatly penciled ledger one evening.

Morgan's solution was her old standby. "I can just borrow—"

"You can't keep dipping into the trust fund, Morgan." His tone was disparaging.

"That's what it's there for." She shrugged.

"But, Morgan, our goal is to function in the black, remember?"

She looked at him sharply. "*Our* goal? Somehow I lost sight of *our* goals. I thought you had yours and I had mine!"

He gazed at her thoughtfully. "Neither of our goals are

fulfilled yet, Morgan. We have until the end of the summer to make them realities. That's what you estimated, remember?"

"But I didn't figure on some of the obstacles we've faced." Her eyes met his steadily. She was determined not to back down in front of him, no matter what her insides were doing. She wouldn't let him know he had bested her in any way, or that she was jelly under all her crusty facade.

"Can't we discuss the business of this ranch without involving our personal lives, Morgan? We have a long time to go yet. And if we can't discuss the ranch, we may as well give up now." His hands shrugged helplessly.

Morgan answered stoutly. "Well, I'm not ready to give up. And I would be delighted to achieve our goals and run this business without getting personal. In fact, I think that was my purpose in the beginning."

Grant's gray eyes darkened, reminding her of clouds over a stormy ocean. "It's too bad you're married to a temporal man instead of a steel robot, Morgan. Then he could easily turn away from you! And there would be nothing emotional . . . nothing personal."

"It's only your heart that's made of steel, Grant! There has been nothing between us but pure, unadulterated lust! Now could we get back to the business at hand?"

He tossed the ledger back on the desk. "Okay. You handle the books and I'll check in with you from time to time. If you have any questions or problems, just ask. I'll do the same. Otherwise I won't bother you. And I expect you to return the favor. I don't want to be stumbling over you every time I turn around. Now, we have six new horses coming in tomorrow and six more next week. They'll keep me busy most of the time. We have to train them and shoe them—"

"Are they broken?" Morgan asked quickly. Even though things were strained between them, she didn't want to face that experience again.

His answer was a curt nod. He turned to leave, then paused and glanced back at her. "Incidentally . . ." He pulled a long envelope from his shirt pocket. "Here's the petition for adoption from the Navajo tribe. It's just basic info about his . . . about you.

138

Would you mind filling it out and dropping it in the mail?" He flipped it onto the desk and was gone.

She looked at the white envelope and burned inside because Grant was so assured that she would comply. Her conscience wouldn't allow otherwise, for she couldn't let David suffer because of matters between herself and Grant. And he knew it. He had the upper hand, and she hated him for that!

Temporal, indeed! Diablo was more apt!

During the next two weeks Grant was occupied with the new animals, as he had predicted. And Morgan spent her mornings going over the accounting and her afternoons planning the activities for the dude ranchers. She visited several other ranches in the area, meeting the owners, making friends, studying their procedures, and merging their ideas with different ones of her own.

So Morgan and Grant managed to stay busy, their paths never crossing, their personal lives never touching except for a terse word occasionally. Morgan lay awake nights listening to the staccato pecking of Grant's typewriter. Many times it clicked late into the dark, lonely nights. Apparently he had decided that being a writer was superior to being a rancher and was attempting to renew his former career. Or perhaps he was preparing for summer's end. Morgan lay awake long after his typewriter was silent, worrying about what time would bring.

A loud pounding jarred Morgan from her nightmare-filled, restless sleep. Before she was fully awake, she was struggling to rise, for accompanying the thunderous noise was Boyd's alarmed call.

"Grant! Grant! Wake up, man! Hey, Grant!"

Morgan's heart pounded wildly, and her hands shook as she struggled with her robe. She first thought it was fire! *Or vandals! Or Willa's sick!* With her imagination running rampant, Morgan stumbled out into the kitchen where Grant was listening intently to Boyd's breathless explanation for the disturbance.

". . . and they busted down the north fence and followed that white devil up into the mountains—" Boyd's words were elaborated by both arms flying excitedly in the air.

Grant's countenance was calm, sleepy. "All of them gone?"

"Yep! Even the mules! They're heading for the San Juans as hard as they can go!" Morgan had never seen Boyd so animated. "And you should see the mess they made of the fence! The *new* fence! We've got to go after them before they get too far ahead!" Eager anticipation of the hunt was written on his wrinkled face.

Grant raised his hands, gesturing for calmness. "Okay, okay, take it easy, Boyd. We'll get them. But, first, let's get organized. Morgan, you make some coffee. Boyd, call the Haroldsons. See if we can borrow a couple of horses. And let's get dressed. It looks like a long day."

Morgan seethed inside as the men left her to prepare the coffee. While they were off taking care of the emergencies, she was obliged to feed them and take care of the kitchen. Well, she wouldn't let them have all the excitement. Quickly she primed the coffeepot, then hurried to dress, colliding with Willa in the process.

"Throw some breakfast together, will you? We're going after the horses!" And she was gone to dress for the excursion. She would show Grant LeMaster!

Morgan stepped out of her bedroom just as Grant opened his door, and they faced each other. She was dressed to the teeth with a shirt, sweater, jacket, jeans, and boots. It was obvious that she didn't intend to hover over the scrambled eggs. For a long moment their eyes met . . . questioned . . . clashed.

"Where are you going?" he growled.

"I'm going after the horses with you," she announced solidly.

"That's ridiculous!" he scoffed. "We've got to go into the mountains on horseback after them. You can't do that!"

"And why not? I'm perfectly well!" Her hands pounced jauntily on her hips. "Boyd certainly can't do that much riding. Don't forget his crippled leg."

Grant's face scowled, and she could see him relenting inside. "Are you sure you're up to it? Are your ribs still bothering you?"

"I'm fine," she half lied.

"It's going to be a hard trip, Morgan."

"You'll need some help. You can't do it by yourself. Anyway, they're my horses, too."

He sighed and, without a word, acquiesced by just leading the way out to the breakfast table. Morgan followed him, satisfied

140

and smug. She had gotten her way . . . and that wasn't easy to do with Grant.

Grant and Boyd discussed the strategy for retrieving the horses around the early-morning breakfast table. The plans, by necessity, included Morgan, as Grant assumed the role of decisionmaker. "Willa, could you pack us some food? Morgan and I will follow their trail into the mountains. Boyd, you take the Suburban and scout the area for any stragglers and the mules. I'm sure they're around here somewhere. They couldn't make it into the mountains at the same speed as the horses."

"You're taking Morgan?" Disappointment was obvious in Boyd's eyes.

Grant nodded, taking full responsibility for the decision. "Yeah, Boyd. I need you to take care of things around here at the Rocking M while I'm gone. You'll have the responsibility of getting those mules back as well as repair of the fence."

"Sure, Grant." Boyd nodded, trying to mask his true feelings. He rose and murmured, "I'll drive over to the Haroldsons now and lead the horses back so you can get started. He said he'd have them saddled. Good neighbor. Said he'd come over later and help repair the fence."

"Good. I want it secure by the time we get back. Eat up, Morgan. We'll leave in about ten minutes. And you definitely need nourishment today." As Boyd left the kitchen, Grant cast an accusing look toward Morgan that would cut steel.

Defiantly she responded to his unspoken blame. "Would you rather take Boyd with you? You can always change your mind."

Grant's eyes touched her flaxen hair, the unusual deep chestnut eyes, her pouting, sensuous lips, and knew he desired her more than any woman he'd known. "Now, you know I'd rather be in the mountains with you. Boyd will get over it. I'm not so sure I will, though." His tone was soft and low.

His expression told Morgan more than she wanted to know. "We have a job to do, Grant. Don't forget—"

"I haven't forgotten *anything*, Morgan."

"Then you'll recall that we decided to keep our activities strictly business." She bent her head to eat the breakfast before her. Even after Boyd's temperamental display and Grant's roguish replies, she was determined to make the best of the excursion.

She would make every effort to prove herself helpful to the men, especially after winning—or was it taking—the opportunity. Stubbornly she admitted to herself that she didn't regret taking Boyd's place. After all, she would rather be active in the search than sit at home and wait for someone else to return her own horses. She longed for the adventure . . . the excitement. Even if that meant following Grant into the mountains.

There was noise outside and she knew that Boyd had returned with the horses she and Grant were to ride. Her husband rose with the admonition that they'd be leaving soon. With one last gulp of coffee she followed him out into the frosty, dark morning. Willa pressed two bulging saddlebags into her hands.

"This ought to take care of you for a while. Are you sure you're up to this, Morgan? It's not too late to back out. Boyd could always go along." She couldn't help hovering just a little.

Morgan shook her head, but before she had a chance to say a thing, Grant moved close. "We'll be just fine, Willa. Thanks for the food. This early-morning breakfast is above and beyond the call of duty, but we really appreciate it. Take good care of David."

Willa's smile of gratitude was grand. "You know I will, Grant. You two be careful and . . . good luck."

"Oh, we'll get them. We can't afford not to," Grant said confidently, swinging his long leg over the horse's back and settling easily in the saddle. Morgan hurried to mount her horse, vaguely noticing the small, tight blanket roll tied securely behind the saddle. It didn't occur to her that they wouldn't be back, with errant horses in tow, before dark.

"See you later." She smiled and waved. Morgan was happily off on the adventure she sought! No more sitting behind the desk all morning!

"Be sure to get that fence fixed, Boyd," Grant called, already fifty feet away.

Morgan kicked her horse and followed Grant's lean, straight back as they made their way into the rugged San Juan Mountains. The Colorado sun sent streaks of light across the trail and reflected a pink glow on a distant peak, but it would be hours before they saw and felt its warm glow on their backs. Up the steep and rugged terrain, down plunging ravines, across natural arroyos, edging narrow trails, farther and farther they traveled, deep into the giant ponderosa pine country. Quietly they shared part of the huge lunch Willa had prepared and placed in Morgan's saddlebags. The sun glowed enthusiastically, lulling them, and Morgan longed for an hour's nap in the quiet, peaceful place.

"Couldn't we stay here for a little rest, Grant? We've been on those damn horses for hours."

He shook his head curtly. "Don't have time. Those beasts haven't stopped, or we'd see signs. They can't just keep going, though. They've got to stop soon."

Morgan sighed with exasperation. "Why are they keeping up such a pace?"

Grant looked at her for a long moment, then a crooked grin broke his straight face. "They are just following their male leader. What's wrong, Morgan? Aren't the mares liberated enough for you?" His wicked laughter echoed off the towering rock cliffs.

Her chestnut eyes narrowed angrily in response to his mocking jabs. "I just thought they'd have more sense than to follow blindly, that's all!" Morgan grabbed the saddle horn and swung herself achingly into the saddle again. She could ride as long as he could, by damn!

Grant moved his mount alongside hers. This time he attempted seriousness. "Are you feeling all right, Morgan? Are your ribs hurting you?"

"Oh, of course not! That's not the part of my anatomy that's hurting!" She bolted out in front of Grant to lead the way. Let him stare at her backside awhile!

Grant's laughter again rocked through the craggy mountains. It was as if they were alone in the entire world . . . nothing or no one to disturb them. . . .

They continued along the treacherous mountain paths for the course of the afternoon, stopping once for drinks and to rest the horses. Grant hiked to a nearby cliff and spent the time looking, never halting his search, even when Morgan slumped wearily against a tree trunk. Then he mounted his horse impatiently, not waiting for her to catch up, but leaving her to struggle alone.

Finally Morgan called to him. "Grant? Don't you think it's about time we started heading home? We have a long distance to cover. It's getting dark and . . . cold. We can get an early start tomorrow morning."

He wheeled around to face her, an amused expression on his square-jawed countenance. "Go back? Do you want to lose them completely? We're not far from them. I just know it."

"But, Grant—" she began.

"We're not going back, Morgan. Pick a campsite."

"Campsite?" she gasped. "Sleep up here?"

He shrugged and again that devilish grin spread across his face. "That's the usual reason for a campsite. 'Course, I'm game for more activity if you are!" He turned his horse and trotted over the next hill and out of her sight, chuckling.

She followed him, still protesting. "But, Grant, we're not equipped . . . and it's going to be cold up here tonight."

Grant had already dismounted in a lovely little glen cushioned by millions of pine needles and canopied by the spreading ponderosa pine branches that stretched upward to the darkening sky. Morgan was taken aback by the gorgeous, quaint place. It was like a dream . . . or a western location from a Louis L'Amour novel. They were all alone and left to the wiles of the mountains. A slight shiver ran through her then, and she could feel Grant's hand on her leg, urging her to dismount.

"Come on, Morgan. We're more equipped for keeping warm than you realize."

She dropped the reins and slid off her horse into Grant's waiting arms.

"Willa packed more food in my saddlebags, and we each have a sleeping bag. As for the cold . . ." His arms tightened around her. "I'll be glad to keep you warm." His head lowered to hers and those lips that had mocked her all day covered hers hungrily.

An inner lament escaped her lips as Morgan responded to his warm kiss, reaching up to clutch his shoulders, involuntarily pulling him closer. Oh, why did she respond so eagerly to him when she hated him so? But she didn't give herself time to figure it out. She was too busy enjoying his touch, his kiss, his warmth.

Grant's lips breathlessly trailed hot kisses down her neck to the pulsating hollow of her throat, and she moaned his name softly. She parted her lips, willingly receiving his gently probing tongue. Voltaic sensations spread through her limbs, exciting

Morgan to meet the depths of his passion. His large hand sought her soft contours, cupping her soft, warm breast under her many layers of clothing, impartially exploring one mound, then the other, until the rosy tips met his palm with relish.

She murmured his name aloud. "Grant, Grant . . . love me . . ." She knew they should stop . . . she should stop this growing surge of electric passion between them. . . .

As if saying his name aloud broke the spell, Grant groaned softly. "Morgan, we've got to . . . make camp before dark. There'll be time for this later." He kissed her lightly on the lips before moving away.

Morgan took a deep breath of the cold, fresh air. As it cleared the sensuous cobwebs that enmeshed her entire being, Morgan wondered what had come over her, responding to this hateful man that way. She certainly hadn't intended to . . . didn't want to . . . Oh, God, what was happening to her? She had to get control of her emotions—and of her actions.

"Gather some firewood, Morgan, while I take care of the horses." Grant called instructions from where he worked to unsaddle the animals.

Orders! Same old Grant, Morgan thought wryly as she bent to retrieve a variety of small kindling twigs and a larger tree limb to keep the fire burning longer. *That's what has happened to me,* she mused. *My love for Grant was ignited long ago . . . even before our marriage. Now, even though I try to turn away from him . . . to hate him . . . one little spark is enough to rekindle my love . . . and desire . . . again. Maybe it's just desire. I know that he has no love for me. He admitted his reasons for marrying me were as far from love as mine were. And he only went to bed for . . . what were his words that night? "Pure unadulterated lust"! And that's what came over me, too. Lust!* Morgan glanced over at the sight of Grant bending to care for their horses. Ah, but he was such a scandalously virile man, it was difficult for her to force her mind from him, especially since she had gone to bed with him. She knew the ecstasy of his warm, hard body on hers, the fire-trails of his kisses, the skill of his lovemaking. Grant had made her think his love was real that night. However because of her lack of experience, Morgan doubted if she could judge his true feelings. He had never admitted any love for her. Not really.

Morgan's breath choked in her throat. *That's because there isn't any love.* Sighing raggedly, she bent wearily to her task, the aches and pains of the entire day on horseback descending on her. How would she fare through the solitary, chilling hours tucked away somewhere in the San Juan Mountains with a man who didn't love her but persisted in stirring her emotions to a boil?

Grant interrupted her meandering thoughts as he gazed in agitation at her small pile of sticks. "Is that all you could get, Morgan? This won't keep the fire going an hour. Come on, honey. Let's get with it! I'll help you."

Honey? Her heart thumped expectantly . . . hopefully . . . sadly.

Together, silently, they worked to build a decent fire with plenty of wood stockpiled to endure throughout the frigid night in the mountains. They ate quietly, yet ravenously, their appetites spurred as much by the cold as by hunger. Near the glowing warmth of the campfire, Morgan huddled on her sleeping bag, its down-filled layers insulating her from the earth's chill. Grant loomed opposite her, perched impatiently on a cold rock, his elbows braced on widespread knees, his eyes dark with desire. He sat hunched like a coiled spring. No words were spoken between them, but the timeless timbre was obvious, the understanding was clear. Evocative tension stretched thin in the mountain air, as tight as a leather strap, wet after a sudden storm. They were alone in the world and needed each other this night . . . for warmth, for protection . . . perhaps even for love.

By the time they finished dry ham sandwiches, water bubbled merrily in the small collapsible pan on the fire. As if that simple chemical reaction were a signal, Grant stood, an impending destiny rising with him. He brought his sleeping bag to Morgan, draping it across her back, letting his hands linger on her shoulders, touching her cheeks lightly.

"Is that better?" His low, sensual voice enhanced the spell that captured them both as silvery, undulating smoke cast about languidly.

Morgan nodded and lifted grateful, mahogany eyes to his, a faint, shy smile on her lips. One look into Grant's taut face, and she knew he was within her power. It was obvious that he desired her tonight. She had only to acquiesce. But did she really want to tease her own emotions again? Did she want to fool herself with acts of love? Somehow as she stared into his smoky-gray eyes, Morgan felt as though she was caught in *his* spell . . . she was instead within *his* bewitching power.

Abruptly Grant turned away from her and stooped near the blaze with a low, aching grunt. After preparing two cups of hot chocolate, he handed one to Morgan, then settled purposefully beside her. He tucked the sleeping bags snuggly around them, cocooning them from the frosty air. Their shoulders and thighs touched, and Morgan could feel Grant's arm move against hers as he brought the drink to his mouth. She smiled to herself when he groaned low and shifted from one aching hip to another. She was experiencing those same pangs throughout her body and appreciated their kindred miseries. It drew them closer.

They drank wordlessly and the tension between them mounted. Why was she being so foolishly mute? She had so much to say to Grant. There were many questions to ask. There should be a lifetime of communication between them. She knew so little about this unusual man she had married. And yet Morgan was captivated by the sweet enchantment of being alone with Grant, deep in the San Juan Mountains. Their hidden little world was lit only by the crackling circle of fire near them. Morgan was lured toward the warm energy radiating from his body, and she longed to feel him against her again.

She attempted to initiate conversation. "Grant . . ."

He turned to her, his gaze lingering on her lips before meeting her eyes with a passion-filled, unasked question.

"Oh, Grant, don't—" Morgan gulped hard, forgetting whatever she had in mind to say to him, knowing what was inevitable.

His lips were close to hers as he murmured hoarsely, "Don't deny this feeling between us, Morgan. Forget our differences tonight."

As his kiss deepened . . . lengthened, Morgan swirled in the lovely magic that ensued. Oh, how she wanted to forget that harsh words had ever passed between them. His lips crushed hers ravenously, blocking out all thought except of the glory of the moment. Responding to her own wild desires, Morgan's arms opened to receive him while her lips parted to ensnare the tongue

147

that sought her sweetness. His hard body stretched out, and he pulled her to match his length.

Once again his hand sought her silky warmth, slipping under her layered clothes and caressing her thrusting breasts and taut nipples. He pressed his palm against her, and she matched his pressure. Uttering a soft moan, she arched toward his compelling touch.

"Come to me, Morgan, my little one . . ." he persuaded, raining her flushed face with kisses. "Take these clothes off. I'll keep you warm . . ."

She struggled, but his leg sprawled over hers, pinning her to immobility. Oh, God, it was hard to think when he touched her like that . . . when he spoke those words. Could she forget—even briefly—that he didn't love her? Could she . . . was it possible to *make* him love her?

Grant's ragged voice whispered in her ear. "Morgan, I want you . . . I need you so badly . . ." His hand slid from her taut-nippled breasts to her waist and unsnapped the jeans. He unzipped her jeans and tried to eliminate their encumbrance.

She tried, futilely, to move away from him. "Grant, we . . . we shouldn't—"

"Shouldn't? My God, Morgan! I'm your husband!" Grant's hand moved roughly inside the jeans he had managed to open, caressing her intimately. Morgan gasped with the unexpectedness of his boldness, giving his other hand opportunity to pull the jeans over her slim hips. "Morgan, don't fight it! I want you . . . and you want me, too, so don't deny it for both of us!"

He was right, and Morgan ruefully admitted it to herself. She allowed him to help her discard the layers of jackets and shirts from her silky bodice. He even strained to remove her boots, then tugged again on her tight-fitting jeans.

"I could stand, you know." She giggled.

"Naw, that would make it too easy," he asserted with a satisfied retort as the cumbersome jeans finally slid free of her legs.

She reached down for his head and ran slender fingers through thick, dark hair, luxuriating in the curls that bent so near to her contours. "Grant, oh, Grant . . . Grant," she whispered, letting his name rustle past her lips.

"My God, Morgan," he rasped with a sharp intake of air as

148

his steel-sharp eyes discerned the pale, exposed image. "You always tear me up when I see you like that!" He gazed, intrigued, as her creamy curves danced with crimson flickers of light from the campfire. Kneeling beside her, he jealously sought her vibrant softness. His hand comprehensively ranged the length of her naked body, exploring from her knees upward to her hips, the warm, feminine juncture at the tops of her legs, her quivering belly, the tender rib cage, tantalizing her breasts' burgundy peaks to fiery firmness.

Boldly she reached for his warm hands, compressing them unflinchingly atop her heaving bosom. "Now it's your turn to undress. We'll both freeze together."

"I'll make sure you aren't chilled, little one," he replied, squeezing her alert nipples between thumbs and forefingers. Small spasms rippled through his muscles as her inquisitive hands pushed the shirt from his shoulders and lingered delicately on the lean sinews that predominated his upper torso.

"Looks like you need someone to keep you warm, too, Grant," she teased. Her hands encircled his throbbing rib cage, forcing his bare chest against hers. With audacious purpose Morgan writhed until her soft breasts were crushed to his solid chest. Her tongue bedeviled his half-open lips as he reached frantically for his belt and those binding jeans.

"Morgan, you're a witch! Hold on! Just wait until I get— Oh, damn, the boots!"

Instantly Morgan was up on her knees. "Here, let me. I'll help you, darling. It's the least I can do since you so courteously divested me!" She grasped one of his boots with fervor and pulled with all her might, but nothing happened.

Grant laced his hands beneath his head and watched the antics of his ivory-skinned wife. "Morgan, you have to turn around with your back to me and pull on the heel. It's the only way to get those tight boots off."

Obligingly she stood, turned her back to him, and hitched up one heavy, booted foot. Taking the heel firmly in both hands, Morgan hefted her weight futilely to remove the offending item. It didn't budge. Once again she pulled. This time something cold and flat shoved against her bare buttock, forcing Morgan, with boot in hand, to stumble free!

"What in hell—" she gasped as she wheeled around, hobbling over the rocks with bare, tender feet.

Grant shrugged, with the most faultless expression he could muster. "It was the only way, honey. I had to help—"

"Damn you, Grant LeMaster! You put your dirty boot on me!" she exclaimed, horrified.

His laugh was a guttural chuckle. "Let me brush it off ... there ... I didn't mar a thing! Smooth as a baby's!" His large hands stroked both rounded buttocks intimately to Morgan's delight, and they both ended up laughing joyously. "Now, the other one, honey. This time, no boot, see?" He wiggled his toes at her, and Morgan knew that unshod foot would be the brace this time.

She bent quickly to grab the other dusty boot, and just as she expected, his bare foot sank into her gently curved bottom. But she was prepared for his thrust this time and shored herself suitably. "Aha!" She held the boot up triumphantly, then tossed it casually with the other. "Now, the only obstacle is this—" Morgan grasped one pant leg, then the other, shifting, scooting, maneuvering, until the jeans slid past his hips and revealed Grant's bulging manhood, still covered with his skintight Jockeys.

Morgan feigned dismay. "Underwear, yet! All right, get rid of those, too! If I have to freeze, bare-butted, so do you!" She made a rapid dive at the sleeping bags and the man she knew would warm her tonight.

Grant shed his underwear and lovingly ran his hands along her shivering body, which was already pressed against his. They came together, breathless and trembling, seeking comfort and intimacy. They were just two people alone in the world, their conflicts laid aside for the night, perhaps forever.

"You're cold," he rasped. "Come on, Morgan. Let's get inside the sleeping bag where you won't get chilled any more."

Suddenly shaking from her exposure, Morgan nodded in agreement. Grant scrambled in first, then slithered Morgan down his length, kissing and teasing her body as she went. With a low, satisfied groan he pulled her onto him, letting the weight of her body excite and arouse them both.

Morgan tormented him with kisses ... his eyes, his cheeks,

his chin, nipping at his lips and neck and chest. Enthusiastically her probing fingers massaged the corded muscles of his neck until he groaned, "My God, Morgan, you're a fast learner. You're driving me crazy!" He rolled them over, cradling her body under his. "This way I can keep you warm all night. I want you so, I could love you all night long."

"You wish!" Morgan laughed as he kissed the wildly throbbing hollow of her throat.

"Oh, God, yes, I wish! Do you want me, too?"

Morgan relished the pulsating desire that rushed through her whenever he touched her, and she arched against his male hardness. "I want your love, Grant. You know I do," she whispered shakily.

"Oh, yes, little one. I can feel it. I want your love, too." His arms molded her to him, guiding her ardently, feverishly, in the ways of love until they both reached passion's pinnacle.

Morgan exalted at Grant's unreserved words of love, as she interpreted them to mean what she wanted to hear. His kisses ignited the dormant flames within her, and she moved seductively against his extravagant blaze of warmth. Willingly, eagerly, Morgan gave in to the age-old glories of loving. Her wild desires matched Grant's that night. They were two lovers lost in their own hidden world.

Later they lay curved together inside Grant's down-filled sleeping bag. "Are you warm enough now, little one?" he murmured against her ear.

"Hmmm . . ." She snuggled even closer, cherishing the way the hair on his chest and belly tickled her back.

His hand feathered her smooth, silken skin. "Ah, Morgan, look at all that we miss by arguing. This feels so good to have you close to me . . . responding to me."

"Um-hmm . . . nice." She cupped his hand over one breast.

"Morgan," he began, his voice suddenly tight. "Something has been bothering me for some time now."

She giggled teasingly. "Why, Grant, that's been settled. That's what tonight was all about."

"No. This hasn't been settled at all."

Morgan turned to lay on her back and gaze up at him. He was serious. "What's wrong, Grant?"

151

His hand rested on her flat belly. "Who is André?"

With a nervous little laugh she asked, "How did you know about him? He's . . . he's nobody."

"Oh, I think he definitely is someone in your past. How important is he to you? You . . . you called his name when you were sick. I thought he'd been your lover but . . ."

Morgan reached up to trace his lips with her index finger. "Oh, no, Grant. No one was my lover before you." She took a deep breath and his hand rose and fell with her ribs. She supposed she had to tell him about André. Now seemed an appropriate time, when she was nestled in his arms, able to let him know that he meant more to her than anyone. "André was a man I met in Europe. I thought I was in love with him. He was very handsome and . . . and we—"

"Morgan, please—"

"It's okay, Grant. I want you to know," she explained honestly. "André convinced me he cared for me, too, and I agreed to become his lover. But he was selfish and rough—not at all like you, Grant—and he left me crying that first night. Afterward I found that he was married! I was very upset, feeling used and manipulated . . . and stupid. I fled to Amsterdam and was staying with a couple who are old friends of my family when we received word of Daddy's death."

Grant's once-relaxed hand had clinched into a fist on her stomach. "Then you came home to the sadness of losing your father and the unfair will," he encouraged.

"Yes. Actually the will stated that if I wasn't married or the ranch wasn't profitable within a year, I would share its ownership with my brothers. But I was too stubborn and proud for that to happen. This ranch was the only property Daddy left me, and I decided I'd be damned before I'd let my brothers take over it, too. So I made up my mind I'd do it myself. Adam had agreed to help."

"But then Adam broke his leg."

"Yes, and you came into my life." There was a smile in her voice. "I must admit, by that time I was convinced that Daddy hated me, and my feelings ran pretty much the same for the entire male species. You included. But I knew I needed help from a man . . . and, Grant, I'm glad I chose you."

152

His fingers roamed in teasing circles around her belly and navel, then slowly lower. "So am I, my little one. So am I." He lowered his face to hers, kissing her completely at great length.

"Now it's your turn," she plied. "Where did you grow up? And what were you doing during those years that I was in Europe?"

His hand stroked her smooth, silken skin and the soft triangular mound. "I was gathering creative experiences for my writing," he murmured, nuzzling her ear.

She wriggled, trying unsuccessfully to escape his maddening manipulations. "Come on, now. The truth—"

"I grew up in Boulder with my grandparents. I left home at eighteen and ended up in Nam. By the time I came back, my grandparents had died. I finished college and did some freelancing for a few years. Then my old college buddy called to see if I'd like to go skiing one last time this season. I said, 'Sure!' Then Adam broke his leg and . . . I'll bet you can guess the rest!"

She placed a smiling kiss against his neck. "I know the rest. Some crazy dame asked you to marry her! Now, tell me about your writing. What are you writing about that takes so much of your time? I've . . . I've heard you typing late into the night." Did she dare tell him that she lay there in her lonely bed, longing for him while he paid homage to that damned cold, clanking machine?

"I'm writing the great American novel," he muttered sarcastically. His hand slipped up to cup her splendid breast, teasing the tip slightly.

"Grant!" His name was a sharp gasp. "Grant, I wonder if you're writing about me . . . about us."

"You?" He laughed. "No, little one. You're my private life. You're too special to share. I want to keep you to myself." His feathery kisses fanned the smoldering embers deep inside her, making concentration on anything outside their sleeping bag impossible.

"I don't see how you can write at night . . . so late . . . after a full day of ranching." She found speaking increasingly difficult when he touched her like that.

Grant grasped her hand and pressed it to him intimately. "I don't expect you to understand, Morgan, but sometimes when

153

I'm writing, I don't know where I am or realize that I'm tired. Writing is my life. I love it and can't seem to stop, even when I've been a wrangler all day."

"Grant—" Morgan's voice wavered as she became acutely aware of where her hand rested and Grant's subsequent masculine response. "Are you . . . are you writing again so you can become independent enough to leave me?"

"What?" He turned to her, his breath quickening. "Whatever gave you such a crazy idea?"

"Don't leave me, Grant," she begged, her hand moving over him of its own accord. "Please don't leave me. . . ."

His arms wrapped tightly around her, pulling her face close to his. "Oh, Morgan, I'm not going to leave you," he rasped hoarsely, desire gripping his body and affecting his irregular breathing. "I want you . . . need you. And I'll be here with you as long as you want me, little one."

He lowered his head and left a fiery trail of kisses from one placid nipple to another until each perked up alertly, meeting his flickering tongue with eager anticipation. His lips adored the entire swell of each breast, over and over, bringing them to firm mounds of burning impatience. Morgan thrust them upward to augment the sensations of his teeth kneading those cherry points ever so gently. Soft sounds escaped her lips when Morgan thought she couldn't bear his finesse any longer.

But endure she must, as Grant carefully brought her to the brink of passion. Again and again he led her to the edge, then allowed her brief relaxation, then seduced her to the razor-sharp edge once more. Each time he lengthened her ascent, heightening her unconstrained longing and enjoying her complete and total capitulation under his tutelage.

Finally, in anguish Morgan cried out, "Grant . . . oh, Grant . . . now!" Her legs crossed atop his. With a soft laugh of satisfaction he pulled her over him, filling her with his love and keeping promises made in the heat of passion. Together they ignited flames of passion that warmed them throughout the cold, mountain night.

"Morgan . . . come, little one," Grant urged. He spent the night gratifying, spoiling, teaching his sensitive bride; and she in turn satiated him, convinced of his love for her.

154

Dawn came chillingly to the inner mountain ranges and Morgan stirred, seeking the warm length that had curled against her nakedness all night.

"Morgan! Morgan! Wake up!"

"Hmmm." She smiled, snuggling for the warm body of her husband.

"Hey, little one! Wake up! I've found them!" His voice was loud but definitely not beside her in the sleeping bag. Morgan opened her eyes, searching. How dare he leave her so cold? "Grant?"

He answered her from across the glen, where he was saddling the horses. "Come on, Morgan! Get up! They're eating in a small meadow about five miles away!"

"Who?" And then she recalled that the purpose for their trek into the mountains was to find runaway horses. But who cared about them this morning? It was much too early. Morgan couldn't bear the thought of crawling out nude into the chilling morning air. Why, she could see her breath in a stream of misty fog! She lay very still until she heard his footsteps approaching.

"Morgan? Are you awake? Hurry up and get dressed!"

She looked up at him in aggravation. "Don't I even get a cup of coffee before I have to climb on that damn horse again?"

His voice was demanding. "No. We don't have time. We'll lose them if we wait too long."

"Grant!" She gritted her teeth and ventured out of her warm cocoon.

He laughed as she tore into the discarded clothes, her bare, shapely legs and hips glowing in the morning chill.

"Don't laugh at me, you beast!" she shouted.

He grabbed her sleeping bag and began to force it into a tiny roll. "Hey, no one would like to stay here better than me! But I'm going after your horses, my dear!"

"*Our* horses!" she flung after him, scrambling to mount her horse and follow him.

"Okay. Let's get *our* horses and go home!" He flashed a marvelous, sleepy grin at her and led the way.

They found the mares grazing contentedly in a hidden meadow. On a rise, keeping watch, stood the magnificent form of the white stallion that had led them astray. He raised his fine head at the first sight of Morgan and Grant. Their presence spelled danger, and with a flash of his tail, he wheeled and galloped up an opposite slope. Nickering to his new mares, the stallion rose, pawing the air, then galloped over the far hill and out of sight.

Grant quickly roped the lead mare and, with Morgan bringing up the rear of the bunch, kept the group together and headed them out of the meadow and away from the wilderness. The greater part of the day was spent leading the mares back to the ranch. Lunch was a brief exchange of food and water, then on toward home.

It was late afternoon when Morgan and Grant finally reached the ranch. Boyd shouted a typical cowboy-salutation and opened the gate to the newly repaired corral. Morgan was numb with hunger and exhaustion and her limbs were weak. Grant reached a supporting arm around her, steering her toward the house.

Willa greeted them on the doorstep, a worried, unusual expression on her face. "Is she all right, Grant?"

He nodded tiredly. "Coffee, Willa. We need coffee, food, and rest."

Morgan smiled faintly at Willa. "I'm okay, just tired. And sore! What I really need is a hot bath!"

Willa smiled grimly and answered, "Sure you do. Supper's warming in the oven. Grant . . ." She placed her wrinkled hand on his arm.

His response was immediate. "What's wrong, Willa? You look —"

The woman's mouth tightened as she nodded to him. "Grant, the caseworker came here to see about David while you were gone."

156

CHAPTER TEN

Grant's hand knotted into a fist as he involuntarily gripped Morgan's shoulder. An angry shadow darkened his tanned face and a muscle flexed ominously in his squared jaw. But in his eyes there was a tinge of fear as he demanded, "She didn't take him, did she? Where is he? Where the hell *is* he, Willa?" He stormed through the living room like a bull elephant on the rampage, arms gesturing violently, calling, "David! David!"

Willa hurried after him, frightened by his sudden, explosive temper. "Oh, no, Grant! She didn't take him. He's over at the Haroldsons playing with their grandson. He'll be back in a couple of hours. Is that all right to let him go to the neighbors' to play?"

Grant turned and stared at her for a full minute, as if determining whether David would be allowed the freedom of playing.

Placing a comforting hand on Willa's shoulder, Morgan gently took command of the uncomfortable silence. "Of course he can go play with a little friend, Willa. That's fine—"

Grant's fury turned instantly toward Morgan. "Who are you to interfere with my son—"

Morgan's steady, brown-eyed gaze bore into him as she met his anger with her own. "Oh, look at yourself, Grant! You're acting absolutely paranoid! Of course a child can play with a friend without cause for alarm. And David is no exception. Now,

Willa, come sit down and tell us all about this caseworker who came here."

Grant clamped his jaw broodingly and followed the women to the seating area, knowing deep down that Morgan was right. He was being an alarmist. This raging reaction was so unlike him. But the thought of losing David . . . that little rascal had wrapped Grant around his little finger—tightly. "Go ahead, Willa," he muttered, trying to regain his control.

"She came about two yesterday afternoon," Willa began. "At first she thought Boyd and I were the . . . adoptive parents. She just sat at the kitchen table and had a glass of tea with us and . . . talked and asked a few questions. She was a real nice lady."

"What kind of questions?" Grant sat tensely on the edge of his chair and leaned his elbows on his knees. Forgotten was the two-day trip on horseback, the renewal of his relationship with Morgan, even his exhaustion.

Willa continued. "Oh, she wanted to know things like how long David has lived at the ranch. And how long Boyd and I have been here. And what we had observed about your family. I guess she was sent to make sure no one was cruel to David or something."

"Damn!" Grant exploded again. "Who do they think we are?" He was on his feet, pacing the floor like a wild man.

And again Morgan intervened. "Grant, calm down! This is perfectly normal for an adoptive child. They question everyone who knows the families. That's usual procedure. It doesn't mean that they think any particular thing is going on with David. It's common to check on them. They have to be very careful in the placement of these kids. You wouldn't want it any other way. It's just that we weren't here, that's all."

"There's one other thing she did ask about, though," Willa admitted.

"What? Asked about what?" It was Morgan this time who jumped. *Damn!* How she wished they could have been at the ranch yesterday to meet that caseworker.

"She asked if you left David in my care often."

Grant raged again. "Well, what the hell does she mean by that? What in the name of the stars was I supposed to do with him? Drag him into the wilderness, just so I could keep him with

158

me? What the hell does she think we do? Leave him all the time? What did you say, Willa? Did you tell her we take good care of him?"

She nodded obediently, quickly, to appease him. "Of course! I told her you always take David with you. That this was the first time you'd left him overnight as long as I could remember."

"That's right." Morgan nodded in agreement. "Including our . . . wedding." She started to say "honeymoon," but caught herself, remembering there had been no such occurrence for them.

Grant's eyes settled on her for a brief, understanding moment, then he smiled defensively. "You're right, Morgan. We didn't even take a honeymoon and leave that kid. I wonder if that would satisfy the Indian agency!"

Morgan turned to Willa. "Is that all she talked about?"

"Well, that's all she asked us. Then she sat with David and talked to him awhile." Willa spoke hesitantly, knowing Grant would be furious again.

And he didn't disappoint her. "Talked to David? What in hell did she talk to him about?"

Hesitantly Willa admitted, "I don't really know, Grant. They sat on the sofa here, and I was out in the kitchen."

"You left him alone with her? And you couldn't hear what they said?"

She shook her head. "But they only talked about fifteen minutes, and he seemed real happy the whole time. She didn't say anything to upset him."

"And then she left?"

Willa nodded again. "But, Grant, before she left, I told her that you and Morgan . . . love David very much. Of that I'm sure."

A curtain of relief veiled Grant's face, and he took Willa's hand, encouraging her to stand. "Willa . . . thanks." He paused awkwardly before repeating, "Thank you. It's . . . it's true, you know. I . . . we love him more than *anything*. And I'm sorry I've been such a jackass today. I'm just tired and . . . worried." His long arm swept around her, and he hugged her long and hard.

Willa's face was flooded with relief and she smiled. "I under-

159

stand, Grant. I'm worried, too. I hope I said and did the right things. Now, how about that cup of coffee?"

Morgan watched them walk to the kitchen, Grant's arm draped over Willa's bent shoulder. She had felt those secure arms of his around her in joy and passion. But could it ever be called love? *Ever?* She was haunted by Grant's emotional confession to Willa. It reverberated in her weary mind: "I love him more than anything." *Or anyone?* she wanted to ask, but didn't dare. Morgan feared the answer.

When David arrived home, Grant questioned him extensively until the boy complained that he wanted to have a snack and not talk about "that lady" anymore. Grant relented but spent more time than usual with him during the evening. When he finally tucked David into bed, he closed himself in his old room. Morgan could hear that infuriating *peck-peck* of the hard, cold typewriter. Frustrated because he turned to that inanimate object instead of her, she curled between the sheets alone. She sank wearily onto the pillow and fell asleep listening to the staccato, rhythmic sound she was growing to hate.

Hours later Morgan was awakened by a scuffling in her room, near her bed—and Grant's plaintive, "Morgan, are you awake?"

"Um-hum," she mumbled, trying to rouse herself. Before she could wake fully, Grant's warm, hard body slid into bed beside her, engulfing her immediately in his sweeping arms.

"Hold me, Morgan. Oh, God, love me . . ." he mumbled into her long, tousled hair as he buried his face against her cozy neck.

Still half-asleep, she reached up, opening her arms instinctively to him. Her heart pounded at the abruptness of the interruption of her exhausted sleep and his earnest request—*love me.*

Ardently she responded. "Oh, yes, darling . . ." Morgan placed eager kisses against his ear, then the dark hair that strayed near her mouth.

Grant didn't lift his face to hers, but continued to awaken her with fiery kisses . . . and his bedeviling, blazing tongue. Quick, sure strokes encircled her breasts, spiraling wildly to the lively, flaming peaks. A gentle suckling immediately brought them to tight, uncomfortable knots. He hastened downward, leaving her

160

breasts burning with unrelenting desire, igniting her navel and flat, tense belly.

Yet on he moved, relentless in his tongue's exploration of her sleep-drugged body. Morgan moaned with the unexpected pleasures that suddenly gripped her as his hands grasped her knees, impelling them apart.

Grant was masterful in his ability to agitate her, tormenting in his drive to intensify her desire for him. And Morgan remained passive, willing to submit to this immobilizing ecstasy. She twisted her fingers in his hair. "Oh, Grant . . . don't stop . . . don't—" she gasped, writhing with the unassuaged tightness that clinched her entire body.

Yet stop he did, giving each firm nipple one last gentle tugging before he crushed his muscular chest against them. His hands gripped her fiercely, raking down her back, reaching for her sore hips and kneading them impatiently against him.

His lips had set a hot trail of kisses across her body, waking Morgan to greater pleasures than she had ever believed possible. Roughly Grant's insolent lips accosted her, tempting her senses, arousing her fiercely. She felt his teeth chafe her own soft lips, while his hands grappled her thrusting breasts, teasing them to ripened perfection. When he forced her to a quick submission, a soft whine escaped her lips, but was lost in Grant's overpowering passion and exultant groan. His lovemaking was rough and abrupt, not gentle and skillful as in the past. He seemed to take his anger out on Morgan physically, as he aggressively took her and made her his own.

Afterward, as the tension in Grant's taut body relaxed against her, he slipped to her side, cuddling while he dozed. His raging passion had left Morgan weak and perplexed, and she gazed, now fully awake, at his shadowed form. Impulsively she ran slender, digging fingertips through his dark hair, spreading her fingers over the noble head that slumped against her shoulder.

She relished these quiet, precious moments alone with Grant and her private thoughts. Without the ever-present passion between them she could honestly evaluate her feelings for him. Her index finger traced his eyebrows, the jet-black lashes curved against high cheekbones, his long, straight nose.

Inevitably he had become her haven of strength. She looked

161

to him for guidance and direction around the ranch. He had, by combination of their marriage and honest, physical labor, unselfishly saved the ranch for her. *For them.* Without him . . . she shuddered at the thought.

And, unexpectedly, he had become her lover. That was the most precious surprise of all. He taught her about loving—physically as well as emotionally. Her finger outlined his well-shaped lips, recalling the ecstasy they had created for her. Just tonight . . . but tonight's lovemaking had been different. Turbulent and stormy . . . almost like their life together. Her hand wrapped around the cords in his neck, easing down to the crisp, curly hair on his chest. She dug her nails into the inky mat, raking lightly with a growing temerity.

Morgan tried to understand Grant's need for punishing . . . for lashing out. She, too, had felt like lashing out when life's circumstances were beyond her control. But she had been rewarded—surprisingly—in one of those instances. Affectionately she ranged the span of muscles that banded his chest, marveling at their masculine shape.

Her reward was her marriage to Grant . . . for this man she had chosen to be her husband had introduced her to loving. Her curious hand followed the ebony, hairy trail that led down the center of his well-formed torso. Morgan was discovering the wonders of Grant's male physique and her own powers to titillate and arouse. It was a wonderful, heady feeling to know that she could manipulate him in such a way. She, too, possessed the skills to captivate him at will, as she had been mesmerized by this virile man in her bed.

In return she loved him—even his savage touch—more than she had ever imagined possible. And she couldn't understand it completely. More times than one she had wondered if his affection for her was merely for someone who filled her needs at the time—whether it was a "wife" in the adoption, or lover in his bed. But no, she had to believe . . . wanted to believe that he loved her.

Shamelessly Morgan stroked Grant, delighting in his response. She needed his love now, not just his angry, raging passion. She wanted his compassionate, abundant love. Swallowing a sob, she turned to him, embracing his sleeping form. He moved instinctively into her open arms, thrilling her with his intimate confirmation of her bold ramblings.

"Ah . . . Morgan . . . you're enough to drive a man crazy—" His voice was a hoarse rasp in her ear.

"I thought you were asleep."

"Nobody with any life in them could sleep through that!"

"Well, how was I?"

"How? Hmmm . . . passable . . ." he growled.

"What?"

"Well, honey, there's always room for improvement—"

"Grant—" Her hand tightened.

His laugh came from deep within his chest. "How about fantastic . . . creative . . . romantic? Come here, I'll show you—"

The assurance of his touch, his need for her this night, his masculine response, gave Morgan peace and a deep happiness that Grant was here in her bed. He was hers . . . even if just for tonight.

The next morning Morgan stirred enough to see Grant dressing in the semidarkness. "Grant?" Her voice was thick with sleep.

He turned to her and gazed solemnly for a moment. "I didn't mean to wake you, Morgan. Go back to sleep."

She smiled serenely at him, remembering their renewed love . . . and the previous night. "Grant, come here . . . please." There was a promise in her tone.

He strode over to her relaxed, inviting form and stood wide-legged, gazing down at her. *God! He was handsome!* "I can't, Morgan. I have too much to do today. I . . . hope I wasn't too . . . rough last night, little one. I don't know what happened to me . . . just lost my control, I guess."

Morgan licked her bruised lips with a frown. Didn't he remember the gentler embrace—the sweet lovemaking? "Grant? Are you all right?"

"Yeah," he muttered, rising. "I have some early chores to do. Later this morning, I'm going in to town to see my lawyer." He walked out of her bedroom quietly, leaving Morgan to wonder and worry in the early-morning darkness.

Why was he going to see his lawyer? Was he trying to arrange to leave after all? He wouldn't leave her now—so close to the opening of the dude ranch! Surely he couldn't just end what they had started of their relationship! Or could he?

By the time Morgan struggled down to breakfast, Grant and Boyd were working in the barn. She tried to catch a few moments alone with him, but he rode to check the far range. There was no time for talking, explaining. Certainly Grant made no moves toward that end. So she watched in dismay and concern as he eventually drove toward town, taking David with him. Apparently he was taking no chances that anyone would check and find that he had left the child again. *Or was he taking David away for good?* Why did that thought always haunt her?

It was with great relief when hours later Morgan spotted the familiar burgundy Suburban drive up and park beside the ranch house. She wanted to rush out and grab them both up in her arms, hugging David's tousled black head close, taking Grant in her arms reassuringly. But she refrained. Instead she watched as they ran chasing each other into the barn, only to emerge minutes later with two horses to saddle. They worked together, then mounted and galloped over the far range, out of sight. They enjoyed each other tremendously and it was plain to see the love from both sides. David idolized his new father. Grant adored his little son. And Morgan was nowhere in the picture.

After dinner Grant followed his usual routine with David. With the playing, the bathing, and the reading behind them, he finally tucked his son in bed and entered Morgan's bedroom. Left on her own, Morgan had showered and was in the process of drying her hair. She was scantily attired in a shortie gown that did nothing to hide her sensuous curves. Her breasts were covered with pale blue net, the nipples hidden by lacy embroidered butterflies. With her arms raised to complete the job of drying her long hair, she made a very alluring picture.

Grant stopped midroom, drinking in the sight of her. He took a deep gulp of air, then turned away from her and sat on the end of the bed. It was as if the sight of her repulsed him, and she was puzzled by his strange actions.

"When you finish that, I'd like to talk to you, Morgan. And put on a robe," Grant ordered.

Morgan halted her task, leaving the hair slightly damp, cascading down her back like a honey waterfall. She walked slowly, deliberately, to stand in front of him. His eyes climbed guiltily as far as those lacy butterflies. Morgan propped her hands on her hips and asked pointedly, "What in hell is wrong with you, Grant? Why are you acting so strange? Coming in here to finally explain what you're up to, telling me to put my clothes on! Usually it's the other way around! You didn't mind taking them off up on that mountain, even at the risk of pneumonia! And last night, in this very room, you were happy to take me au naturel!"

Grant's cloudy gray eyes traveled from her face back down to those butterflies, and involuntarily he reached for her. But he was slow and Morgan easily stepped out of his reach. His eyes sought hers, almost pleadingly. "It's hard for me to talk to you when you're . . . like that, Morgan. My God, woman, I'm only human! And you're . . . very alluring. It's almost a sin for anyone to have such dark brown eyes when everything else is blond."

Morgan wheeled toward the closet. "Sorry, that's just the way I am. You have to accept me like this." She grabbed the satiny robe and wrapped it around her tightly. "Okay, everything's covered. So talk."

Satisfied that she had covered herself sufficiently and he could try to concentrate on what he had to say, he began. "As I told you this morning, I went to talk to my lawyer today. And I'm going to need your help, Morgan."

Morgan's heart beat rapidly, fearing what he would say next. Hadn't she helped him enough? Hadn't she done his bidding as a wife? And more! What if he wanted her to cover for him while he took David far away! *Oh, dear God, No! Don't leave me now!* She tried to keep her voice steady and calm. "What kind of help, Grant?"

"We've got to stop this bickering and present a loving family atmosphere at all times."

"What?" Morgan's head whirled with the incoherence of his words. "You're not leaving?"

He ran his hands through dark, disheveled hair. "Leaving? Why would I do that? I told you I needed to stay. Listen, Morgan, I've got to remain here and see this adoption through. It's the only way I'll get legal custody of David. This place and . . . you . . . are my only chance. And I need your help."

Relief flooded through Morgan at his commitment to staying —and his admission of needing her. All she wanted was to hear him say that he was staying. Now that he had fulfilled her hopes, she wanted to wrap her arms around him and tell him she would do anything to help him—anything at all! Instead she restrained herself with a quiet, "What kind of help do you need, Grant? Money?"

"Money?" he expounded in disgust. "If that's all I needed, there'd be no worry. No, what I must have is a little more complicated than that. According to my lawyer, we have to look like an ordinary, loving, happy little family trying to adopt a kid."

Falteringly she said, "I . . . I thought we were that already."

"Ordinary? Ha! Happy? Hardly!" His words were scornful and cruel. "We're anything but an ordinary family, Morgan! Surely you realize that!"

"But I'd like to think there's love—"

"Love?" he scoffed. "With all the fighting we do?"

"But, Grant, that's over—"

He shook his head. "For now maybe. For tonight. But what about tomorrow . . . or next week? It's on again, off again, and that just won't do. We need a unified front."

"A . . . unified front?" Morgan gulped. It sounded like he was outlining strategy for a war. Maybe he was.

He nodded. "That's exactly it, Morgan. The caseworker will be back, you know. She'll come unexpectedly, unannounced. Just like the last time. We'll never know when she's going to pop in. But next time I want your assurance that you'll be . . . that you'll help me . . ."

Morgan's voice was hollow as she finished his statement. ". . . by being your 'loving wife.'"

"Exactly. If they suspect trouble in this marriage, or—"

Morgan interrupted. "—or an arranged marriage . . ."

Impatiently Grant seethed, "Oh, come on, Morgan. Surely we're beyond that now. I just want to put away our battle gear. After all, we've shared a very intimate relationship. Doesn't that mean anything to you?"

"What does it mean to you?" Morgan's voice was quivering, matching her insides.

166

"Morgan, we've lived together for months now. We've slept together. You know me."

Morgan's voice was barely above a whisper. "I hardly know you at all, Grant." She didn't like the way this conversation was going.

Grant was on his feet, pacing, expostulating loudly. "You know that I love that boy. You know that I'll never let harm come to him, and I'll be the best parent he could ever have. Do you realize what will happen to him if they take him away from me? From us? He'll become a ward of the state, tossed from one place to another. That is if they can find a foster home who'll take a kid his age. Otherwise he'll remain in an institution. I'll do *anything* to keep that from happening!"

"Anything?"

"Anything!"

Morgan raised her chin defiantly, afraid to ask—knowing the answer. "Would you even go so far as to sleep with me to establish a 'loving relationship'?"

His eyes were steely gray and his lips thin. "If I have to."

"You bastard!" she exploded with deep inner anger and pain. "You slept with me just to gain an intimacy to bind us together purely for your own needs! You tried to make me your 'loving wife' because that's what you needed for David. You never really cared about me."

Painful realization spread across his face. "You're wrong about that, Morgan."

"Wrong about what? That you never loved me? That all you care about is yourself . . . and that kid in there? I think, for the first time ever, I understand you and your motives! I really know you tonight!"

"No, Morgan—"

But she wouldn't be stopped. "You cared nothing about me! Or about my feelings!"

Grant's slate-gray eyes narrowed. "Morgan, I've helped you this entire summer. I've worked my butt off for you and put this ranch in order. You've got to admit, I haven't shirked my end of the bargain. The dude ranch opens next week, and by damn, we're ready. The building, the trail rides, the big barbecue, the singing around the campfire, the horses are broken—everything is ready for guests! The very least you can do—"

Morgan interrupted. "Never mind that I've given you and your son a home and warmed your bed during all this!"

He spread his hands in explanation. "What I need from you now—"

"I know. You need a unified front, a certain loving appearance from me, not a warm bed. Well, let me remind you, Mr. LeMaster, the bargain included fifty thou at the end of the summer, not a 'loving wife'!"

"Morgan—"

"Listen to me for a change, Grant! Just shut up and let me have my say in this!" Morgan folded her arms and paced in front of the contemptible man she called her husband. "I'll agree that you've done a remarkable job on the ranch this summer. Without you I could never have done it. And I appreciate that. But things are different now. Different from what I thought they were between us. Actually I also fear what would happen to David without us because, believe it or not, I care about him. Since I know that you love him, I will be a part of your unified-front idea and play the role of your 'loving wife.' I will do my part to help you become the legal father."

"Oh, Morgan—" His voice was raspy.

Her tone was hard and firm. "I'm not finished, Grant. I'm doing this for David, not you! And you won't have to sleep with me anymore to manage that feat. I will be the epitome of your loving wife, but you will stay away from my bed. That's not necessary anymore. And I won't be used any longer!"

"Morgan, surely—"

"If you come near me again, I'll scream the whole sordid tale to the Social Welfare departments of Arizona and Colorado! And to the Navajo Tribal Council!" Her chestnut eyes narrowed. "You stay out of my bed. Agreed?"

His gray eyes seemed to shoot daggers at her. But Morgan was strong in her conviction. She met Grant's gaze steadily and stood firm before him. She would not back down now. If he wanted something else from her, he had to give up something. And apparently her love was not high on his list of priorities. Therefore she would eliminate it.

"Damn you, Morgan," he muttered gruffly. "Agreed!" Then Grant turned on his bootheel and stalked out of her bedroom for good.

Angrily she tore the loving ring from her hand and flung it tearfully against the door.

CHAPTER ELEVEN

The glorious warm weeks of the Colorado summer passed busily. The opening of the Rocking M Dude Ranch kept everyone hopping, including the four newly hired ranch hands. Weekends were unbelievably busy, with "ranchers" filling the guest bunkhouses and activities filling every waking minute. To the public Grant and Morgan presented a beautiful, loving couple, hard at work and deeply in love. There was laughter, light kisses, frequent touching of arms and shoulders for everyone to see. They were a fun-filled, delightful addition to the dude ranch experience, and most people left with promises to return again next year. Some even made reservations. Morgan's financial statement moved rapidly to the black.

For all the loving facade Grant and Morgan exhibited, there was no affection when no one was looking. Grant disappeared whenever there was a spare moment into his room to type.

Morgan closed her bedroom door and sat alone to brood silently. She ached for a kind word or touch, but received neither from Grant. Many times she wished she had never banned him from her bedroom. She longed for his touch, his warm body next to her, even though he didn't care a damn about her. And yet Morgan was sure she couldn't live like that. She knew she was only torturing herself with those thoughts, but couldn't help it. She loved him deeply, and it was tearing her up inside. She was willing to do almost anything for his love.

How many times had she gone to the bedroom door, hand on the knob, preparing herself to tell him she didn't care what he thought of her if he would just come and hold her through the night? And yet each time she lost the nerve it would take to do it. And she knew it would just destroy her even more to know that he took her to bed and still cared nothing for her. So, morosely, Morgan went to bed alone, listening to that goddamn, clanking typewriter late into the night until she fell asleep to its rhythmic beat.

"Grant, she's here." Willa's quiet voice interrupted his poring over the books in the study.

It was one of the few quiet days they had enjoyed since opening the Rocking M. The time off would be spent, as usual, getting ready for the next "ranchers." Morgan had asked Grant to review her figures before she made a trip to the bank. Grant, lost in the realism of credits and debits, murmured, "Hmmm? Who's here, Willa?"

"That woman who came before. David's caseworker."

Grant's head snapped up and his attention was immediate. The late-night hours he had been keeping were taking their toll on him. His eyes were bleary and his face showed signs of strain. A brief glance out the study window, and he muttered to Willa, "Why isn't she coming to the front door? Where the hell is she going around the side of the house?"

Willa smiled and shrugged. "Maybe she sees David and Morgan. They're in the corral, practicing roping."

"Roping? My God!" Grant rolled his eyes and moved hurriedly through the house.

The woman propped her arms casually on the fence railing, watching Morgan and David's antics. They were unaware of anyone's presence so far and, like two children, were taking turns trying to circle a post end with an unwieldy rope.

The woman turned, smiling, as she heard Grant approach. "I think David's at least as good as she is." She laughed, amusement lighting her dark eyes.

"At least," Grant agreed, chuckling. "Before long he'll be teaching her."

"I wouldn't doubt it at all. David seems capable of doing

171

anything he sets his mind to. You must be Grant LeMaster. I'm Cora Whitefeather of the Navajo Agency Branch of Welfare. I'll be reporting on David's case to the Tribal Council in Arizona." She extended her hand to him and he shook it, liking her informality instantly, in spite of himself.

He nodded. "I'm Grant LeMaster. Nice to meet you, Ms. Whitefeather."

She smiled graciously. "Please, call me Cora. Is this your wife with David?"

"Yes, that's Morgan with David," Grant said, watching with satisfaction as they laughed and played together. Morgan was certainly keeping her promise about being the loving wife and mother. She actually looked like she was having fun.

It was a few more minutes before Morgan spotted their audience. She waved and Cora returned the gesture.

"Come on over, Morgan!" Grant called, beckoning. "This is Cora Whitefeather, David's *caseworker.*" His emphasis was implicit.

Morgan smiled warmly and extended her hand. "So nice to meet you. And I understand you've met David." Her eyes sought Grant's briefly. Their "unified front" was in force!

Cora smiled and exchanged greetings with Morgan, then turned her attention to the boy. "Hello, David. Do you remember me?" Her raven eyes matched his, and the resemblance of their shared heritage was obvious.

David grinned confidently at her and nodded. "You're the lady who was going to bring me a white feather, just like your name. Did you bring it?"

"David . . ." Grant looked uncomfortable.

However Cora Whitefeather adeptly ignored Grant's discomfiture and acknowledged the child's request seriously. "I wondered if you would remember it, David. I brought you a beautiful eagle feather today. It's in the car. Come with me, and we'll get it." David accompanied her eagerly, leaving Grant and Morgan to gape nervously at the two bronze-skinned figures.

"Grant, I like her. She seems very nice. And she obviously cares for David," Morgan said when they were out of earshot.

"Obviously. But don't forget why she's here, Morgan. Her job is to find out whatever she can about us!"

172

Morgan's reply was acute. "She's here to make sure this is the best home for David. She is not our enemy. Give her a chance, Grant."

His face was taut as he murmured through clenched teeth, "*You* give her a chance, Morgan. I'm prepared to be more realistic!"

"There you go being paranoid again. Take it easy, Grant. We're working on this thing together, remember?"

He nodded tersely as Cora and David approached, chattering happily. "David and I will show Cora the stables and horses. Why don't you make some coffee for us, Morgan? And maybe a little lunch." His affable smile flashed white teeth her way.

Morgan returned his smile with a warm expression of her own and acquiesced agreeably to her husband's suggestion. But she burned with frustration down to her toes as she watched Grant lead Cora to the activity centers of the dude ranch while she was again relegated to the kitchen. She slammed the kitchen door and jerked the parts of the coffeepot into action. Trying to speak calmly, her voice squeaked and she stopped to clear her throat before starting again. "We'd like some lunch, Willa. And do we have any of that coffee cake left?"

"I've already made sandwiches. But the cake is frozen. I'll stick it in the oven right away. It'll be warm enough by the time they've toured the ranch." Willa eyed her young boss skeptically, fully aware of the strain this visit was creating in both Morgan and Grant. Things were not exactly right between them, but she just couldn't figure out what it was. Maybe it was just all this adoption business.

Morgan answered tensely, "Yeah, and I'll bet Grant will be as nervous as a caged tiger by the time he's toured the ranch with that woman. He's already so irritable no one can stand him."

"He is a little tense, isn't he?" Willa agreed.

Morgan sighed. "He's a regular coiled spring, Willa. I just hope he doesn't say the wrong thing and offend Cora today with some offhand remark."

"Oh, he won't do that, Morgan. He knows this visit is too important." Willa confidently patted Morgan's arm.

"Too important . . ." echoed Morgan as she turned to slice fresh celery.

173

Without further comment they prepared the simple lunch. Each was lost in her own thoughts as to the consequences of the caseworker's visit and the adoption hearing. Of course Morgan knew that even if they were awarded custody of David, that would not end the turmoil between her and Grant. With a heavy sigh she tried to force her thoughts back to the present.

Lunch was kept lively solely by David's enthusiastic participation with their guest. Cora had proven her caliber by remembering to bring him the feather. She was obviously interested in him and, typically, he eagerly took advantage of her attention.

Morgan and Grant were gracious, smiling—and tense. They tried to pretend to be completely at ease, but neither was a very good actor. Cora Whitefeather's alert eyes assessed the couple. *She knew.* She had seen those same taut faces before, as prospective adoptive parents tried to be calm in her presence. And she smiled inside. It was a good sign.

As they finished the meal, Cora took the initiative. "David, why don't you run along and play while we grown-ups have another cup of coffee?"

Run along and play? No one ever told him that! David looked up at her, clear disappointment in his dark eyes. He glanced quickly at Grant, who nodded affirmatively.

"You could practice the roping and get a jump on Morgan," he suggested.

"Yeah!" Renewed interest lit his small face.

"And we'll check to see how good you are before I leave," chimed in Cora with a smile.

"Okay!" With a scuffling of chair and feet David left the room.

There was an uncomfortable silence broken only by the tinkling of someone's spoon stirring coffee.

Grant finally spoke, his voice low and strained. "You wanted to talk?"

Cora sipped her coffee, then, "Yes. I want to assure you of a couple of things. One is that even though I'm definitely looking out for David's welfare, that doesn't mean I'm against you two as the parents at all."

Morgan squirmed, but dared not look at Grant as Cora reiterated Morgan's earlier statement.

Cora continued in a serious voice. "I'll admit I am very con-

174

cerned about this child who so far has been deprived of a normal childhood. That doesn't mean he was without love, but we know he was quite isolated living with his grandmother. Now special care and education will be needed to acquaint David with the real world. Then there is the fact of David's heritage. That must not be ignored. It's quite a challenge."

Grant rushed to the defense of the child he loved. "Cora, let me assure you I'm willing to accept any challenge where David's concerned. I know he has some problems. And I'm willing to give him whatever he needs—and more! And that includes all the love he can handle!"

Cora smiled tolerantly at his outburst. "I believe you, Grant. And I can see the loving relationship he has already developed with you and Morgan. And I like what I see."

"You do?" Morgan asked eagerly, almost childishly. She was so anxious that she could hardly think straight.

"I do. And that's what I'm going to report to the Navajo Tribal Council." Cora paused, waiting for the effect of her words to sink in.

Morgan found her voice first. "You are?"

"Yes. And I don't see any problems delaying this adoption. Now let's say good-bye to David. I have a long trip ahead of me."

Bubbles of giddy joy and laughter filled Morgan with effervescence and she was vaguely aware of her own impulsive giggles. Grant was pumping Cora's hand, mumbling hoarse words of thanks, and Willa was clapping her hands in the kitchen, where obviously she had overheard every word.

Wisely Cora moved ahead, leaving Grant and Morgan alone for a brief, exuberant moment. Their eyes met, hers brimming with tears of joy. His arm encompassed her shoulders, squeezing her to his warm chest. His voice was husky. "Did you hear that, Morgan? We've done it! It's almost over! Thanks, honey! I'll never forget it. You gave it your best shot—and it worked!" He removed his arm as swiftly as he had engulfed her and was gone.

Morgan stared silently after him, the tears spilling over and rolling down her cheeks. A huge knot formed in her throat, choking normal breathing. *Damn you, Grant LeMaster,* she thought morosely, *I gave it my only shot! I love him, too! Don't you know that by now?* She breathed deeply several times, open-mouthed, trying to move that choking knot.

"Are you all right, Morgan?" It was Willa.

Morgan turned away and wiped the tears away quickly. "Yes, I'm fine," she managed, and headed out the door. With a sinking heart she knew the answer to her own question.

Within a month David's adoption hearing was held in Durango's old courthouse, via transfer of jurisdiction. It was almost anticlimactic. Of course it was more official than the verbal promises of Cora Whitefeather and her follow-up letter, but they had known. Willa and Boyd accompanied Grant and Morgan, sitting grim-mouthed while David squirmed on the hard bench between them. In accordance with the laws governing the Navajo tribe, Grant and Morgan LeMaster were awarded custody of David. The joyous occasion was celebrated at Swenson's with four ecstatic adults and one raven-haired, brown-skinned little boy toasting spoonfuls of Hot Fudge to Raisin Rum, Bubble Gum to Pistachio.

Yet the jubilance that Morgan felt was clouded by inner turmoil as she wondered what would happen to them now. She just couldn't escape the claws of apprehension that tore at her insides. After all, summer was almost over, and their agreement had been fulfilled. What she hadn't bargained on was falling in love with Grant and his little son as well.

Another week passed before the roof caved in on their uneasy, contractual marriage. Willa and Boyd had taken the day off, their first in many weeks. Morgan was poring over the books, as was her usual morning habit. She reached absently for the ringing phone.

The voice was obviously long distance. "Hello, there! Grant LeMaster, please. This is Jack in L.A."

Morgan wrinkled her brow . . . *Jack?* "I'm sorry, but Grant is out somewhere on the ranch right now. Can I take a message?"

"You must be his new bride I've been hearing about! Tell him I called and he'll be glad to know the deal is set. He'll need to be here in L.A. by Friday to sign. Have him return my call and we'll work out the details." The voice was exuberant.

"Uh, Jack . . . who?" Morgan's mind puzzled over his voice and name. Neither sounded at all familiar.

There was a slight pause. "Just tell him Jack Myer called, sweetie. He'll know."

"Jack? What deal?"

"Didn't he tell you? That sly devil! He must have wanted to surprise you."

"Yes, that sounds like him. Are you going to tell me what deal?" Morgan snapped, perturbed by the glib tongue of the caller.

Another slight pause. "Uh, I think I'd rather not, my dear. I'll let your hubby disclose the little surprise. But don't worry. It involves a great deal of money. I think he'll be happy with the deal we've set. And you will be, too."

"Money?" Morgan's mind whirled. *Gambling?* What the hell was he talking about?

"Just have him call me."

"Yes. I will." Morgan dropped the phone into its cradle, an ominous chill of dread spreading from her scalp downward over her body. Hugging her arms closely, she rocked back and forth slightly and watched the first yellowed aspen leaves of autumn float languidly to the ground.

After lunch Morgan waited until David had eaten and dashed off to play before approaching Grant. "Who is Jack Myer?" she asked bluntly.

Grant was caught off guard and raised his eyebrows curiously. "Jack?"

"Jack Myer called from L.A. Now, who is he?"

He shrugged and spread his hands innocently. "He's my agent."

"Agent? I didn't even know you had an agent."

"Well, Morgan, I didn't think it necessary to explain all of my business to you. So far it hasn't mattered."

"Now, obviously, it does. Jack says the deal is set, and you are to fly out to L.A. by Friday to sign. You are to call him for details. Does that make sense to you?" Morgan's voice was tinged with anger, for none of it made any sense to her.

Grant smiled eagerly at her words. "It certainly does. He's been trying to sell my screenplay for a movie. Sounds like he did it! This is great news, Morgan. Looks like things are working out!"

Icily she asserted, "Things are certainly changing. What else have you lied about in your life? Maybe there's a wife and kids somewhere I don't know about, and you didn't bother to tell me because it didn't matter until someone found out."

"That's a hell of an accusation, Morgan. What's gotten into you?"

"I . . . I feel as though you've led a double life. One that we see . . . and one that creeps out by bits and pieces."

"Don't be ridiculous, Morgan. I don't have any more secrets. No other wife! No other kids! I'm just a screenwriter who happened to get mixed up in a crazy marriage scheme, the likes of which I could never have created in my wildest imagination!" His words were stinging.

"You're not at all who I thought you were—"

"What's wrong with you, Morgan? Afraid you'll be left out of a chance to travel? Miss some excitement? Well, don't worry. I'll take you and David to L.A. with me."

Numbly she answered, "My business is here. I have 'ranchers' coming through September."

He shrugged angular shoulders in a noncaring attitude. "We can make some kind of arrangements. Cancel the weekend or something."

"Cancel? You know I won't do that!"

His slate-gray eyes cut into her. "Look, Morgan, David and I are going to L.A. by Friday. I have business there and I'm going to take care of it. You can tag along if you want to, Morgan. I don't give a damn what you do."

Morgan felt as though her feet had been knocked out from under her. Grant was missing her entire point. He was raving about some damn trip, while she was upset over the continued revelations. *What next?* "Grant, I really don't know you. I've lived with you, been the loving wife you needed for David, even slept with you—and I don't know you at all. At each turn it seems I'm finding out new and different things about you that I never realized. Now with this . . . screenplay thing—"

He interrupted cruelly. "What difference does it make, Morgan? I did your bidding! Even in bed!"

She ignored his reference to the bed. "What difference? I thought you were a free-lance writer. I thought you did travel

178

articles and human-interest stories about the Indians. You . . . you deceived me."

"Look, Morgan, I'll admit I led you to believe I was a free-lancer, but—"

"That's exactly what you told me when we first met! A free-lancer! You lied to me then. And you haven't stopped lying yet!"

He tried to explain, but it was too late for justification. "Morgan, I don't go around blaring to the world that I write screenplays. In fact I was a free-lancer for many years. At the time it was an easy answer."

"An easy answer!" she mocked. "To find out you've been writing plays and negotiating movies while all the time I thought I was doing you a favor by hiring you and providing a home for David . . . It's just too much." She shook her head as much to clear it as to get things straightened out in her mind.

"Morgan." His voice was gentle. "You have done us the greatest favor you could ever do! You played the best acting role I've ever seen as loving wife and mother to David. Without you it would have been hell for me to get custody of David as quickly as I did. It probably would have taken me years. I will never forget it, Morgan. I can't tell you how much I appreciate it. We both do—"

"Acting!" Morgan's voice was shrill. "Don't you know—yet —that I wasn't acting? Don't you understand that I love him, too?"

"Morgan, you're getting hysterical."

But he couldn't hush her. "Why—why couldn't you tell me about *anything*? Your writing . . . your life? After all, I am your wife!"

"Wife?" he jeered. "Hell, we haven't lived together as husband and wife for weeks! You can't claim intimacy. You knew I was working on a project. Surely you could hear me typing. But you never cared enough to ask me once about it."

She nodded and murmured in a toneless voice, "I heard you typing every night . . . every night . . ."

Grant moved to the telephone. "I'm tired of this lashing out at each other, Morgan. If you'll excuse me, I have some calls to make. Should I include you in the reservations?"

She turned her back to him. "No. I belong here, not in L.A."

His words were emphatic. "David and I are going to L.A. with you or without you!"

Her tone was dull, lifeless. "Then go ahead. You never really cared for this ranch . . . or me. You have a different kind of life to lead."

She could hear him step closer to her, but she kept her back to him. "Does that mean what I think it does, Morgan? Without you? Is this it?" His voice was flat with the realization.

She shrugged, her shoulders looking small and burdened. "You certainly don't need me to run your life. You have all you need from me."

"Looks to me like it's mutual, Morgan." Grant grasped her elbow tightly and turned her around to face him. "You don't need me, either! And summer's over."

Her bronze eyes narrowed, carrying all the spite she could muster. "Oh, how I hate you, Grant LeMaster! You'll do anything to get what you want! You are undoubtedly the most ruthless man I've ever known! Why, you even surpass my own father! You both used love to get your way!"

"Don't try to lay that guilt trip on me, Morgan. You used me too, don't forget. You got what you wanted. So did I. Now I have everything I want. So David and I will get out of your life. No more demands, no more deals. Incidentally, about the money . . . just keep it. Maybe you can buy a few more unbroken horses and find some fool to risk his neck to break them for you!"

Morgan's face stung with the hot lash of his words. "Grant, surely—"

His squared jawline was etched menacingly in her view. "While we're gone, go ahead and file for the divorce, Morgan. I'll do nothing to stop you—or interfere with your life again. Just don't interfere with mine." He released her elbow and shoved her away roughly. Reaching for the phone, Grant began to dial.

But Morgan didn't stay long enough to hear him reach his destination. She ran blindly outside, ending up at the barn. Impulsively she threw herself astride a mare, bareback. She rode hard, the wind stinging her tear-streaked face and whipping her long tresses out in a golden stream behind her. Finally, breathlessly, they approached a stream and she allowed the animal to slow naturally. They followed the stream at a walk, both heaving for breath. This was the same mountain stream where she and David and Grant had fished . . . and laughed . . . and loved. And she despised Grant for all that he had done to her life. At one time she had thought he could simply solve her problems. But, oh, how he had complicated things. Now she knew what the end of the summer held for them all. They would part. They would be a little family no more. And David . . . David . . . oh, God, what would happen to him? Whatever did, she wouldn't be a part of it. Oh, how could Grant do this to her? Didn't he know it would tear her apart? But what did she expect? She had known—felt—all along that the man she had chosen for her husband wouldn't stay forever. Why should he? There was nothing more for him. And he was right. They both had what they wanted . . . what they had bargained for. And now what? Grant had said it. *Divorce!*

Morgan glanced down at her hands and the green and silver Thunder Mountain turquoise sparkled—the ring with the legacy of love. What had Grant said that day so long ago when he placed it on her hand? *The one who wears this ring will be forever loved.* Tears filled her eyes, and she knew the legend was false. "We could make it happen," he had said.

Wrong again, she thought.

181

CHAPTER TWELVE

The evening sun was dipping low and an autumn chill was in the air when Morgan arrived back at the ranch. The first thing she saw was the open-doored burgundy Suburban, ready for loading. A large brown box was already tucked in the back. *The toys!* So soon? They were leaving so soon? Morgan walked slowly, wretchedly, toward the ranch house.

Inside the kitchen things were in a general uproar. Willa and Boyd had returned and both were questioning Grant at the same time. David was hopping around the kitchen like a little brown frog. *What a circus!* she thought dizzily.

Morgan touched Boyd's sleeve. "I left Lady in her stall, but she needs to be rubbed down. I rode her pretty hard. Would you take care of her for me, Boyd?"

When David caught sight of her, he flung himself against her, hugging her legs and exclaiming, "Oh, Morgan, please come with us to California! Why don't you want to come? We're going to have so much fun!"

Morgan's hands caressed David's raven hair, and she wanted to cry . . . to wail. Never did she think she would ever be so attached to a child . . . but this one was different. He was special . . . like Grant. And she had helped Grant fight for him. "I . . . I just can't go with you David," she mumbled, glancing at the boy's father. But Grant kept his head turned, eyes averted from hers.

"I'll go take care of Lady," grumbled Boyd. "Would you like to go with me, David?"

"Yeah! I've got to tell my friends where I'm going! Do you think they'll miss me?" He hopped beside Boyd, taking his gnarled hand.

"Sure they will." Boyd attempted a smile.

"Don't forget, I've got your favorite chicken-noodle soup for supper, David." Willa was wringing a dish towel nervously.

"And the cookies! You promised chocolate chip cookies!" David reminded her with a huge smile.

"Oh, yes, the cookies," Willa muttered weakly as they trotted out the door.

"Well, I've got some more packing to do," Grant announced gruffly and strode away quickly.

Willa's sorrowful eyes met Morgan's.

Morgan blinked and propped her fists on her slim hips. "And I've got some talking to do. Take your time with those cookies, Willa." She took a deep breath and stalked off, following Grant.

His bedroom door was open and Morgan glanced furtively inside, gathering her strength for what she had to say. Grant was flinging clothes haphazardly into the open suitcase on the bed. His face was taut, his angular jaw set squarely. He moved with jerky, angry motions.

Morgan took a deep, sobbing breath. "Grant, don't do this. Don't . . . take David away from us . . . from the ranch. I love . . . him."

He didn't even pause in what he was doing. "Morgan, you knew this would end."

"I didn't know anything of the sort! At least I hoped not," she declared. Suddenly her tone was hard, tinged with viciousness. "Have you forgotten that I was also awarded custody of David? If you take him away from me, I'll sue you!"

Grant's tone was low and cruel. "It'll be a vicious court battle, Morgan, because I'll fight you. Don't—don't drag David through that. Not after all he's been through already."

Morgan blinked angrily, knowing deep down that she could never make David suffer through a lawsuit, as much as she wanted to cling to him. She was bluffing, and Grant knew it. She

183

turned away from his steel-edged glare. "You're right, Grant. I could never take him away from . . . his father."

She kneaded her sweaty hands together nervously and felt the ring. *The loving ring!* She jerked it off her third finger and whirled around to face him. With hand outheld she charged sorrowfully, "Here's your ring, Grant. Maybe you can get your money back. The legend lies. There's no love connected with it."

Grant stared at her, obviously shaken, for long moments. It was unutterably quiet. There were no words, only eyes meeting in sad expressions of lost joy. Then he looked down at her outstretched fist holding the ring. His large tanned hands, both of them, enclosed her small fist, keeping it knotted tightly around the legend ring. "Yes, there is, Morgan. The legend doesn't lie." His voice strained to speak normally. "The ring was given to my wife. Keep it as a reminder of my love, little one."

Morgan's heart pounded wildly and her head reeled dizzily for a moment. "What are you trying to say?" she rasped.

He cleared his throat and his voice sounded more reasonable and strong. "I'm saying I love you, Morgan LeMaster. I'll admit, I hadn't planned on falling in love with my wife, but it happened. The ring is a symbol of my love. You can do with it what you will."

His hands still held hers securely, warmly. "Why didn't you ever tell me you loved me?"

He sighed. "You didn't give me a chance."

"I . . . I begged for your love." *Oh, Grant, did I ever tell you that I loved you . . . ever?*

"You had my love, but you twisted it, then rejected it. These separate bedrooms were your idea, you know."

Morgan smiled weakly, agreeing. "I thought . . . I thought you didn't love me. I didn't want to force you into sleeping with me anymore."

"Forced to sleep with you? My God, Morgan! It was all I could do at times to keep from breaking the wall down to get to you! To touch you! These last few weeks have been hell!"

She smiled broadly at the mental image he created. "I . . . I wish you had. I . . . wanted you so much. I hated the sounds of that damned typewriter so late at night. I'm afraid I fell in love with my husband, too."

He placed her hands on either side of his neck and pulled her close. "What fools we've been, Morgan. Look at all the loving time we've lost arguing and . . . sleeping apart. Oh, God, Morgan, I love you so much!"

She hugged him closely, joyously inhaling his musky masculine aroma. "I've missed you," she whispered.

"I've missed you, too. And this . . . and this . . ." He kissed and touched her intimately. "And this . . ."

Morgan arched against him and stood on tiptoe, tilting her head back to greet his longed-for kiss eagerly. His lips crushed hers breathlessly in a sweet, delicious, probing kiss. When he finally lifted his lips to kiss her cheeks and nose and eyelids, she murmured, "Oh, Grant, I do love you. *I love you!* Don't ever . . . ever leave me!"

"Oh, no, Morgan. Never. You and David are going to L.A. with me . . . but we'll postpone that trip at least another night. We have some catching up to do!"

"If we all leave, what will we do about the dude ranch? We're expecting guests."

He nuzzled her ear. "To hell with the guests. We'll arrange something for them. I want you with me. And when we get back, we deserve a honeymoon. How does Cancún sound?"

"Sounds wonderful!" She pulled her hands between them and slipped the loving ring back on her third finger.

Grant held her fingers admiringly, then kissed the beautiful ring and her fingers lovingly. "You will be forever loved, little one. I promise. We can make it happen."

Morgan kissed him boldly. "Now! Let's start making it happen now, Grant. You said yourself that we have a lot of catching up to do!"

"But what about David? And Willa?"

Morgan kicked the door shut. "Don't worry about them. Willa's letting David help her make cookies. If we're not back soon, she'll know what to do." Morgan smiled confidently.

"Well, if that's the case." Grant swung Morgan up triumphantly in his arms. "Let's catch up! What a sweet, sensuous, little wife you are, Morgan! Someone must have taught you well!"

She laughed and kissed his neck. "The best!"

He carried her over to the small bed, and with one nudge of his boot the suitcase slipped to the floor, scattering Jockey shorts and T-shirts over the floor. But the mess was ignored. There was a lifetime ahead for cleaning up the messes. Right now it was time to catch up on love!

LOOK FOR NEXT MONTH'S
CANDLELIGHT ECSTASY ROMANCES ®

When You Want A Little More Than Romance—

Try A Candlelight Ecstasy!

Dell **Wherever paperback books are sold!**

SWEET WILD WIND

by Joyce Verrette

In the primeval forests of America, passion was born in the
mystery of a stolen kiss.

A high-spirited beauty, daughter of the furrier to the French
king, Aimee Dessaline had led a sheltered life. But on one fateful
afternoon, her fate was sealed with a burning kiss. Vale's sun
bronzed skin and buckskins proclaimed his Indian upbringing,
but his words belied another heritage. Convinced that he was a
spy, she vowed to forget him—this man they called Valjean
d'Auvergne, Comte de la Tour.

But not even the glittering court at Versailles where Parisian
royalty courted her favors, not even the perils of the war torn
wilderness could still her impetuous heart.

A DELL BOOK   17634-4   ($3.95)

At your local bookstore or use this handy coupon for ordering:

 DELL BOOKS   SWEET WILD WIND   17634-4 $3.95
P.O. BOX 1000, PINE BROOK. N.J. 07058-1000

Please send me the above title. I am enclosing $ _____ (please add 75c per copy to cover postage and
handling). Send check or money order—no cash or C.O.D.'s. Please allow up to 8 weeks for shipment.

Mr./Mrs./Miss _____

Address _____

City _____ State/Zip _____

Seize The Dawn

by Vanessa Royall

For as long as she could remember, Elizabeth Rolfson knew that her destiny lay in America. She arrived in Chicago in 1885, the stunning heiress to a vast empire. As men of daring pressed westward, vying for the land, Elizabeth was swept into the savage struggle. Driven to learn the secret of her past, to find the one man who could still the restlessness of her heart, she would stand alone against the mighty to claim her proud birthright and grasp a dream of undying love.

A DELL BOOK   17788-X $3.50

At your local bookstore or use this handy coupon for ordering:

Dell   DELL BOOKS
P.O. BOX 1000, PINE BROOK, N.J. 07058-1000

SEIZE THE DAWN   17788-X $3.50

Please send me the above title. I am enclosing $ _____ (please add 75c per copy to cover postage and handling). Send check or money order—no cash or C.O.D.'s. Please allow up to 8 weeks for shipment.

Mr./Mrs./Miss _____

Address _____

City _____ State/Zip _____

Desert Hostage

Diane Dunaway

Behind her is England and her first innocent encounter with love. Before her is a mysterious land of forbidding majesty. Kidnapped, swept across the deserts of Araby, Juliette Barclay sees her past vanish in the endless, shifting sands. Desperate and defiant, she seeks escape only to find harrowing danger, to discover her one hope in the arms of her captor, the Shiek of El Abadan. Fearless and proud, he alone can tame her. She alone can possess his soul. Between them lies the secret that will bind her to him forever, a woman possessed, a slave of love.

A DELL BOOK   11963-4 $3.95

At your local bookstore or use this handy coupon for ordering:

Dell

DELL BOOKS   DESERT HOSTAGE   11963-4 $3.95
P.O. BOX 1000, PINE BROOK, N.J. 07058-1000

Please send me the above title. I am enclosing $ _____ (please add 75c per copy to cover postage and handling). Send check or money order—no cash or C.O.D.'s. Please allow up to 8 weeks for shipment.

Name _____

Address _____

City _____ State/Zip _____

The phenomenal bestseller is
now in paperback!

HOW TO
MAKE
LOVE
TO A MAN
by Alexandra Penney

Over 6 months a hardcover bestseller—"the
sexiest book of the year."—*Self Magazine*.
And the most romantic! "Pure gold . . . your
relationship with the man you love will be forever changed!"—*Los Angeles Times*

A Dell Book $2.95   13529-X

At your local bookstore or use this handy coupon for ordering:

DELL BOOKS   HOW TO MAKE LOVE TO A MAN $2.95   (13529-X)
P.O. BOX 1000, PINE BROOK, N.J. 07058-1000

Please send me the above title. I am enclosing $ _____ (please add 75c per copy to cover postage and
handling). Send check or money order—no cash or C.O.D.'s. Please allow up to 8 weeks for shipment.

Mr./Mrs./Miss _____

Address _____

City _____ State/Zip _____